The Speed
of Angels

The Speed
of Angels

Manu Bazzano

PERFECT
EDGE
BOOKS

Winchester, UK
Washington, USA

First published by Perfect Edge Books, 2013
Perfect Edge Books is an imprint of John Hunt Publishing Ltd., Laurel House, Station Approach,
Alresford, Hants, SO24 9JH, UK
office1@jhpbooks.net
www.johnhuntpublishing.com
www.perfectedgebooks.com

For distributor details and how to order please visit the 'Ordering' section on our website.

Text copyright: Manu Bazzano 2013

ISBN: 978 1 78279 193 5

A CIP catalogue record for this book is available from the British Library.

Design: Stuart Davies

Printed and bound by CPI Group (UK) Ltd, Croydon, CR0 4YY

We operate a distinctive and ethical publishing philosophy in all
areas of our business, from our global network of authors to
production and worldwide distribution.

O Lord,
Nourish me not with love
But with the longing of love
(Ibn al-'Arabi)

They say the darkest hour
is right before the dawn
(Bob Dylan)

I

Wide awake in the dead of night, I call an *avatar* who does not answer. Genet was right: we converse with the dead. We write for the dead in the theatre of memory, the soul's irrelevant domain. For the dead I lie awake at night, for a handful of sardonic shadows on the shores of the River Styx. For a mirage, for a dream I dream up this wounded speech in the dark.

Awake at night, I stare at the ceiling and dig up a primal verse: *The triumphant athlete defeated his opponents at Olympia and was then floored by the gaze of a young woman* – read long ago to my father who was alive then, and who, alive, smiled the smile of the accomplice.

I remember the dream I just had: walking up and up through Trastevere in a heart-drenching drizzle, then getting lost in Piazzale Garibaldi, insolent with the vanity of victory and with a lover's despairing graffiti on the wall. I was going over in my head what I'd say to you, *Life is but a shudder of eyelids do you agree?* You'd understand. Summer would come back on earth.

Is this what insomnia is, not leaning on anything? Insomnia as the cure from metaphysical slumber, from the placebo of theories and the credulity of action, from the vanity of happiness and the alleged superiority of ataraxia. Before it became a drawback, philosophy was this for me once: refusal to rely on anodynes, not wanting to sleep on it.

Awake at night, loitering with intent in the land of the shadows, I seriously consider if I should rent a semi-detached in hell: is this what insomnia is?

* * *

My partner is asleep beside me. From love we learn duplicity.

After all, loyalty belongs to patriots, to those who trade the blessed *earth* for a nasty *soil*, and brandish in a rowdy wind-faded banners made with the discarded shirts of some rich bastard. They love their soil, patriots: hear them spluttering their drunken tunes to Gaia, foolish goddess, benign Theilardian and Lovelockian organism magically rising one day (so they say) from her stony slumber, opening herself up at last to Spirit after centuries of ethnic cleansings, wars, gang rapes and shallow graves offered to the volcanic sun of the future.

Gaia? No thanks. Mother Earth love? Fuck off. The earth is vertigo, wide expanse scattered with exiles, fateful locus where you can't build a dwelling, let alone call anything *mine* – the blue planet whose strange sweetness tricks the blood and every summer makes us sick with yearning.

I turn the pillow. Sleep has vanished. At dawn I will hurl my body into a ravine.

* * *

It's All Saints' night, before the dawn of the Day of the Dead. Darkness came down on our privileged hemisphere, our vision darkened by pain, by a heartache that dissolves the human face into a virtual *avatar*. I am thirsty, thirsty for summer springs. In the thick suburban silence where slumber weaves the dense chimeras of progress and history for the sole benefit of sleepers, I drag my feet, looking for a glass of water.

I remember it now: I had set myself the task of telling what I had learned, of clarifying *sotto voce* at the edge of a bed the compendium of my traveling years, an abstract of fictional philosophy woven between theory and biography. Maybe that's what I'll do. The night is long. I'll do it in our Vulgar Latin, I'll do it in this rented tongue, stepmother tongue, forgotten tongue. I'll do it in this Madonna/whore tongue, plum juice dripping from dark skin, a fruit worshipped to silent ecstasy. I'll give it a try, just to kill time: it will be the distillation of the error that was this wayward life; a bundle of fragments between despair and the vain hope of the world becoming a musical room, as envisioned by that young rogue from Charleville.

A great part of my sleepwalking compendium will be mere theory, I'm afraid. Yet theory is for me play, not foundation: maybe a dance, interrupted by your handwritten words, the only ones in this electronic liaison: *I'd like to be alone with you, shrouded in silence here and now...as slipping slowly underwater...the sound of your voice is supreme.* I was touched, and forgave the cheap mysticism in that 'here and now' and in that exaggerated 'supreme' I fastidiously perceived the ruinous fall that always follows the hyperboles of love. I answered as a scheming schoolboy: *your bite on my lower lip, the brush of a flower.*

I'm thirsty. My chest aches. I'm thirsty for summer springs. I remember it well now: it's a daring feat for a client of mine to simply get out of the house and drag himself to the park in the pale sun and remain there seated on a bench to observe the to and fro of the cheerful shipwrecked in the quiet desperation of a London afternoon.

Never before had I been met at the airport by someone holding a sign with my name on it. Didn't notice at first. Went here and there, shocked by the heat. Then with our greeting we reassembled an androgynous creature. My friend Stephen told me months later that on his arrival in Korea he too had been met by a woman whom he later married and with whom he lives after thirty years.

* * *

Last Wednesday in a crowded tube at six in the afternoon in

the belly of my city I already seemed not to feel anymore the pain that made its home in my chest *(how could we, darling, and why?)*. I am grateful to work, I am thankful to *Ananke* goddess of necessity whom Freud believed antithetical to Eros and the pleasure principle. I perceive in my love of work the scent of salvation, a hope born out of the union of love and necessity, Eros and Ananke, pleasure and reality. Or you can make art out of life, summoning private, transient deities to your rescue: young Mahler, whose piece in D minor for string quartet mercifully filters in my memory; Oscar Wilde, because like him we all are brokenhearted clowns.

Transferred from one prison to another on 13th November 1895, and kept there waiting at the central platform at Clapham Junction (where I find myself every Wednesday on my way to work), Wilde was handcuffed and in tatters, poor Oscar, brought there suddenly from the infirmary and without warning. When people saw him, they just laughed, and when they recognized him, they laughed louder. From two to half past two he was held there waiting for a train next to two policemen.

* * *

Wide awake in the dead of night I prostrate one hundred and eight times towards the East, to Quan-Yin who aids sea travellers in the storm, appears as a maiden to those thirsty for love and also as sister death to terminal patients in overcrowded hospital corridors. I prostrate to the South to my dead parents who conceived me on a night in June (fatal, hermaphrodite month, month of Hermes and Aphrodite).

I prostrate to friends and foes of my hometown, to past loves of whom I ask forgiveness for having thought that this last craze was a first love. I prostrate to you, dream creature whose teachings now obscured by pain, I will no doubt decode one day. It doesn't matter if it'll be too late, if a cruel twist will have had the upper hand, as in a badly written novel. You see, monsieur Genet, just like you I converse with the dead, I call them to behold this fragile life exposed to the vagaries of fate, since there never ever was on the blue planet a more diaphanous existence than the life of philosophers...

* * *

At times I find solace in the melancholy of absence. The heart decelerates after the fury and the heat.

And how strange that everyone, from self-righteous blasphemers to court poets, all grow silent when they listen to Bach or smell fresh bread. The angel becomes human, gladly decelerates his flight to a standstill and burns his lips with hot coffee on a winter morning. Humans amuse him – he is moved by our plight of Buddhas asleep on a bed of roses and thorns.

But you cannot, oh no, hear me, you can't go smoothly into that dark night, you can't with a light heart go and meet the dark dark night, you cannot with a gentle heart go and meet the dark death that at every tolling of the bell, at every toll comes nearer. *Can't hear no bells,* your voice on the phone from the warmth of your kitchen and I heard mockery in your voice as I stood on the bridge stunned by love and a gust of wind listening to Big Ben at seven pm, cut in two by contrapuntal memory – in two places at once and the icy wind feeding on my cheeks. I just stayed there as a biblical stone listening to Big Ben, listening to time itself as Heidegger did, listening to time like the old mother in my client's tale:

"I gathered from our conversation with my mother that she had spent most of her day just staring at the clock! So I thought, She just stays there, resigned, waiting for death. And my son on our way out whispered to me, 'You know, Mom, grandma's breath smelled like grandpa's before he died.'"

I silently return to bed and listen to her breathing, her whom I betray every minute with my thoughts. I listen to the breath of the one who truly loves me with a love I cannot match because more than anything I love this longing to which I stupidly gave a name and a face, rather than loving its pure song as it's done among authentic troubadours. Can't sleep, that's what it boils down to, and tomorrow having sold love to the Pharisees I'll run breathlessly along the river, a condemned man, and hang myself before the seven o'clock news because it is written in the scriptures.

* * *

A flower bloomed in our breast on a day of iridescent calamity (Friday 13 in the Anglo-Saxon world is bad luck but not in the *Bel Paese*, once cradle of the Renaissance and now dazed in front of government TV channels). This transient blooming of ours wasn't conceived in divine screenplays, karmic laws or Akashic records, oh no, nor was it a fruit of Turkish, Chinese and Sicilian fatalism. *I'll* tell you where our ridiculous encounter was written: in the disorderly classifieds of blind biology, in the blind Darwinian wallowing of blood pursuing its inane course in the wheel of living-and-dying. In the pages of airport bookshops' good reads, *that's* where our beatific/idiotic encounter was foretold, my ex-darling. Wait, mustn't give in to the pull of cynicism which from Socrates onwards has been the weapon of the mediocre and embellishes today the new evolutionist Oxonian creed in a world bereft of God, Buddha and crystal gazers.

A philosophy compendium? The journal of a post-modern sailor? You must be kidding...

I shiver at the sight of two nineteenth-century silhouettes in the room where I come to sit so as not to disturb my partner's sleep. In the frail shadow before the Day of the Dead, sipping *Courvoisier* in the plain delirium of this prolonged wake, I recognize Lou and Fritz sitting on the sofa, shrouded in the darkness of this interminable night.

They caution me with their silence. They tell me that a love chained with knowledge and discipleship is doomed from the very start. Lou admired Fritz but ended up mistaking the thought of the eternal recurrence for the accidental revival of metaphysics, the muddled discovery of a myopic Columbus. The beautiful Lou was running away from love (run baby run) and from her prescribed role as Zarathustra's disciple and companion.

There is no peace anywhere in this endless night. I take my leave from the eighteenth-century pair and walk towards the bedroom. On the staircase, I stop. A scene seizes me, cruel and clear. I see a bookshop in Lucca on a distant summer evening; I see a copy of *When Nietzsche Wept* by Irvin Yalom. I dry my eyes (no more brandy, for heaven's sake), and recall with a grimace that I had not forgiven Irv (and had told him so during a brief correspondence) the reduction of a genially perverse thought to the rank of psychoanalytic *noir*. But on this night where nothing escapes the clutch of darkness I make amends and bow to his perseverance, to his existential rendering (in our era of philistine pragmatism) of the irreducibility of the *Joyful Science*'s great jester.

Motionless on the stairs, shrouded in autumn darkness I incongruously recall the laughter and sadness evoked in me when I read *The Schopenhauer Cure*, the other philosophical novel by good old Irv Yalom. But here, you see, things get sticky. Because, you know, he's writing about sex addiction. Now lying on my bed I pull up the blanket and a shiver hits my lower belly... The prince claims your lips, your mouth, your hands. Above all it claims the velvet lady, the slow entry right inside the gate. Uncensored and cold to my entreaties he proclaims: *I want to surge inside her mouth like a spring from a Buonarroti statue.*

This fire inside made me dance when walking through the summer avenues. *Here too is summer at last* I recited, a poetaster in shorts, dreaming oat flakes for breakfast and the caressing voice of one born in the afternoon of a spring day in the island pillaged by Saracens and Turks and never surrendered to eruptions. Life comes back every spring; soldiers die and are buried; on the third day new loves spring up with the anemones and the scent of caponata and the stubborn gaiety of genistas.

Yalom writes of one who cures sex addiction through philosophy. Not just any old philosophy, mind you, but Arthur Schopenhauer's, the grumpiest of all philosophers. I have no idea if in the Italian Boot the notion of 'sex addiction' exists. I lost the grip, my thermometer slipped from my coat pocket in the crowded train of exile. Sex addiction would mean, let's see, resorting to sex in order to buffer one's anxiety and the very uncertainty of life. And so you catch yourself on a sweaty bed, in hyperventilated and salacious embrace; later, while getting dressed, you patch up the embarrassment with verses borrowed from the *Baci Perugina* candies: *Uno dei benefici dell'amicizia è di sapere a chi confidare un segreto* (Manzoni). *Doubt thou the stars are fire... But never doubt my love* (Shakespeare). Following famished and sterile intercourse & platitudes murmured in the prehensile, ungrammatical ardor that demands the world and ends up with dust, you find yourself more *creature* than ever, more mortal and alone than ever in a world meanwhile grown colder and more banal. The respectable yet inexpensive tombstone will read, *He enjoyed a good fuck.* And the same, as Irv has it, could be said of his dog. Perhaps this is what uninhibited sexuality means to the average Italian, for he inherits an unbroken lineage from Gaetano Rapagnetta, who traded his farcical name ingloriously rhyming with the scurrilous *pugnetta*, with 'Gabriele D'Annunzio', the archangel of bad breath, bad teeth and martial posturing, down to *Il Duce* and the *Cavaliere*. And does the Beautiful Country have *any* notion of Schopenhauer, especially after the bad example set by Leopardi who morosely embraced the deterioration of the will preached by the cantankerous Teutonic – Leopardi, who married with zeal both the pessimism and the bitter diatribes against life?

What's more, the distance from fatigued, satisfied Italic senses to sheer dejection is very brief indeed. I have read all the books and so forth. And that a fictional character in contemporary California manages to sew up shreds of his sanity by using Schopenhauer – is that a sign of the times? I may be speaking from puritanical frenzy, or from the regret for having lost an imaginary Eden (*how could we, darling? tell me*), but the idea that others enjoy life doesn't bother me, quite the contrary. I care more for liberty, however, than mere pleasure: to disentangle myself from the clasp that divides and detains, from stupefied hedonism wedded to pessimism of action, from the atrophy of will cloaked as religious decorum.

Could this explain why a people so diversely shrewd and bright have then put up for decades with a succession of rulers straight out of third-rate operetta? Marcuse would have explained such a phenomenon in terms of *desublimation*, of a loss of conscience coupled to the 'happy consciousness' that follows the attainment of simulated freedoms. Sated and befuddled by assorted anesthetics, we agree to infamy and monstrosities dished up daily with bread and *Nutella*. Mind you, Marcuse knew nothing of the new generation of pissed-off pajama-clad hordes, the sofa-bound revolutionaries and inheritors of that prime motor of modernist imbecility answering to the name of F.T. Marinetti, (whose idiotic 'Futurism' badly hid from the start the crudest fundamentalism), those deluded souls who 'explore' the social jungle armed with mouse and laptop.

How to justify the fact that a people with so many emigrants all over the world are then so intolerant towards those who manufacture a possible survival and venture on the sea and drown on the shores of the Adriatic? How to justify the total absence of civic responsibility, the betrayal of the Hippocratic vow transmuted in espionage against illegal immigrants? How to justify the absence of communal feeling and of community itself? Detained inside the diving bell of the *I*, armed with a mouse, a keyboard and a set of headphones, weaving networks of virtual non-encounters. Singles of the world unite. Oh yeah? But relating is painful; after the ecstasy comes the agony; after the laughter, tears; and after orgasm the tears, the tears of Eros. Detained in the diving bell of the *I* my avatar meets yours. Tonight I don't remember your face. The human face draws attention to what we wish to hide. The human face is the beginning of ethics and love. Our own face is alien to us, subject to change, caught by surprise in a mirror, in a shop window. If one had to wear a mask by law, to show one's face would be a daring and uncommon act of trust, the beginning of ethical and erotic exploration. And you? You sealed the end by wearing a mask on *skype*.

I look for you through the mazes of the virtual world, through the hyperactive, desolate hysteria of *second life*. I look for your avatar and mourn the loss of the human face. I am in mourning for the disappearance of the human face in present-day relationships. I weep for the concealment of the body, this inconvenient, late-Romantic artifact, once sovereign of love affairs before the advent of global capitalism.

Got nothing to teach you, you said, *at the most, information technology.* So I became your disciple. You initiated me into the I.T. magic thanks to which we could be reachable every day, every hour. You initiated me to the artificial delight of a disincarnate voice, to the immediacy that burns natural distance between beings. But you didn't teach me how to fathom the presence of your avatar. What does a wretched man do during the interminable night in a London suburb? He switches on his laptop; the warm glow of the screen sends waves in the dark, while he reads the electronic mail of a summer now remote. *I am tired of these toys – mobile phones, text messages, skype – they make me dependent...they trick me into thinking that there are not thousands of miles between us...they trick me into thinking that you and I share everyday reality...I am in pain, but I respect my solitude.*

* * *

What has changed since then: I look at the sky more often; I speak to distant voices with *non-chalance* and punch numbers with managerial ease. I would know how to conduct telematic adultery. What has changed: I look at the sky, southward; I speak to distant voices while my surroundings fade.

Detained in the diving bell, removed from contiguous phenomena, from the *dharmas*, from the teaching of the ten thousand things, from everything that generously sustains me, I erase myself from my surroundings. Hermes, once messenger of the gods – his sublime mission as a postman now perverted by the dictates of egoic power – poor Hermes walks with difficulty but I make out his wings from under a frayed pair of trousers.

The ancient Hermes, when he still was the gods' messenger, warned Ulysses before he went to visit Circe: "Watch out," he said, "make sure you unsheathe your sword; make it gleam in the morning sun." Hermes invites man to not forgo male dignity; he reminds us that the meeting between the sexes is a necessary dance of love and hatred and that to forget this is naiveté. But the Italian male is a straw man, a rapagnetta, the shadow of a man vacillating between ostentatious machismo and complete abdication to the feminine (since he believes woman to be 'spiritually superior'). He cannot avoid being devoured by the Great Mother; Kali will spit out his bones in a football stadium after the unmediated collision and the wheezing intercourse.

Look at the suicidal squandering of the great patrimony of the Italian political left, once the most hegemonically 'Gramscian' in Europe, yet the most impotent and invertebrate left the world has ever seen. From Berlinguer to D'Alema to Veltroni and Bertinotti, a rosary string of nauseatingly obsequious abdications to the Great Mother, Catholic and corrupt, and all in the vain hope of obtaining a tiny slice from a cake already salivated in the foul jaws of Andreottian and Craxian mastiffs.

Immediacy (absence of mediation) has been for centuries an obstacle to the growth of love. Foolishly we entrust ourselves to the cold flame of passion where love is mutual consummation and finally turns into the *perverse intimacy* of hatred: possession of the other, isolation from the world (*what did you see of my world, what did I see of yours?*), ecstasy metamorphosed into exhausted futility, the creaking gates of hell wide open, where fault always lies with the other.

You can't *live* in ecstasy. How soon roses wither... An erotic-religious view of existence is an infernal vision, a place that quickly turns from total freedom to complete dependence. Without mediation and a common venture, love is mere passion, nuptials of moods marinated in despair. This pointless exchange of ill-combined instincts confuses Eros with carnality, with the idolatry of the body now converted into flesh; gobble it quickly before the onslaught of entropy. I had dreamt of taking you to the temple of Taoist love...we opted instead for the brief and desperate flight into the hyper-real.

What makes love last? Do I have even the right to answer? Can Judas pontificate on the secret of disciplehood? But I will do so complacently and with the tenderness of fresh wounds suffered and inflicted. Here is what I have to say, hear me out, will you: ahem, the first requisite for love to endure is not to run away from difficulties. Big fucking deal I hear you say! But wait, listen to me: the honeymoon cracks up sooner or later and the night sky smears itself with the colours of the bittermoon. Get it? I'm not talking about the skirmishes of litigious love, of the bittersweet refining of palates that keeps spiritual diabetes at bay. Not at all, I am talking of the *bittermoon*, the menace banned from poetry anthologies and from Valentine who was a martyr by the way and not a Hollywood star or some Nureyev. I am talking of the profound need to smear oneself in ashes and diligently chew one's own shadow and – even *more* difficult – chew and swallow the shadow of the loved one. Such passage is oblig-atory, I'm afraid, and no discipline (philosophical, religious, amorous, you name it) can afford to ignore it. No birth happens without blood, sweat and tears and it's a fatuous aesthete (one who gives aestheticism a bad name) a father who refuses to be present with eyes wide open to the birth of his little one, why he is a right ponce in my humble opinion, a rapagnetta who flees from the pain implicit in all relating.

Without the bitter moon, love is infatuation, fatuous flame that zealous bonking on beds and inside vehicles does not transmute but precipitates instead in mere fatigue. Oh yes we have tasted the vinegar on the cross: it was the other's cold sweat. We recoiled from it in disgust, seeking refuge within the armor of self-love and the shield provided by that renowned Italian vice, wounded vanity, *egoisme a deux*: mutual infatuation – beautiful, sumptuous – journeying through the spasms of bad poetry, lasting the time of the silly season.

This caustic self-reproach is already, I feel, a pathetic plunge into the swamps of rationality. I find myself already emulating that eminent couple of slapstick buffoons, Socrates & Plato, the Laurel & Hardy at the dawn of the provincial world of philosophy, cradle of this Western world of ours which survives egregiously in our privileged hemisphere alternating deeds of heroism mixed with bouts of tenderness & idiocy, all veering towards an apocalypse always fashionably late in coming. Why is it late? I'll tell you why: because the apocalypse is immanent, darling, it's here, ever present, punctuated by every ticking of the clock. This is why I must resort, in the end, to the drug of the terminally fatigued: reason. I chastise my own pride for having engineered my own imprisonment in the net of an infant Dionysus, for having been deaf to the teachings of a mature Dionysus, to the sensual lucidity that I believed I had absorbed from Goethe. But it doesn't matter: last night I danced to Scarlet's violin in Dylan's *Hurricane*...

Thing is I'm fed up with you, fed up with every bloody reference rotating around you. I am not being a good disciple of Heraclitus and Nietzsche, am I? To the eternal and discontinuous flow I'm juxtaposing pathetic musings of cut-rate eternalism. And here's a confession: I want to re-live *ad infinitum* that handful of hours spent with you, give the Nietzschean eternal recurrence bad publicity, selling it cheap to those imbecile interpretations that read it as upside-down Platonism, aesthetic hunger of beautiful, revealing moments. Yes I would want to live again its pains, the pain of that handful of hours, thus reasserting the frightening authority (existential, not metaphysical as Heidegger had it) of the eternal recurrence of the same and absurdly reasserting also this love that carries on, this incurable love that goes on (and on). No escape from the eternal recurrence: its ingenious (mythical, literary) proof is Freud's *Unheimlich* (untranslatable, like psychoanalysis) and the compulsion to repeat. You yourself have confirmed its bitter truth, by re-enacting with me your ancient plot, the vicious circle of an infernal deity: *I carry in my heart the beautiful moments.* Oh yeah? And what about the *ugly* moments, eh? What about the not-so beautiful moments? What about the cyclical drama of beauty and the beast? What about going around in circles in the circus of *samsara*?

Cut a long story short: a) every being and inanimate object projects a shadow; b) if we fail to recognize this, we end up roaming eternally within the confines of the metaphysical fairground in search of sublime candy floss or, c) befuddled and desublimated in front of a screen owned by a bejewelled tycoon and where every foreign film is dubbed. Or, d) we end up munching bread and Nutella in the peremptory darkness of the Mediterranean evening or, worse e) we end up rehearsing lines lifted from *Hobbes for Beginners* in order to shock naïve liberals at dinner parties. In such condition of extreme de-*privation* – gift of the *private* property – we communicate with a splintered world while seated on the decomposed wings of a gargantuan dozy Hermes.

Open-minded bloke in his forties with GSOH would like to meet woman or couple for adult fun. Triumph of Marcusian desublimation; annihilation of the opposition (cultural, political, of feelings): happening everywhere you look, including within Italic Buddhism, a mere extension of magical thinking, exotic furnishings in the safari of one's own epidermis. The statue of Gautama as an item in the shopping list, his potentially devastating influence thoroughly sanitized. Once upon a time receiving a Buddha statue as a gift meant having to rearrange the design of a home if not rebuilding it from scratch. If not giving it up altogether and becoming homeless. Could it be the same with Christian faith as well? I can see how in Kierkegaard faith is fatal adventure, vertigo and despair: I do not recall similar responses during the sluggish hours of catechism. Unless one is willing to repeat the experience of Jesus, existentialist hero *par excellence*, who only on the cross became the Christ through the *lamma sabachtani*... Unless one is willing to experience Søren's painful renunciation of his love Regina in a nineteenth-century Copenhagen and in the name of an absurd longing for the absolute... But faith is now a Sunday pastime, obsequious humming from a shady larynx, at times a croak from a double-breasted suit. Same goes for Eros: love is not acquisition or decoration. Eros is a god, a reckless mendicant who wrenches your guts before you can say *hi*: That's why we sing his praises in love anthologies and, beset by his ascendancy, pull back in quiet recollection embalming the 'beautiful moments' for our retirement years on the Riviera; that's why we exchange Eros for generalities.

You have betrayed love, my short-lived-darling, you betrayed it for a generality: by diverting at first its blinding light into your daydreams of carnality; by placating the obscure gyrations with the palliative of pleasure; by shrinking its magnificence into yet another signpost en route towards the isolationist advance of an I. Straight on, third on the left. It is humiliating me to see Eros reduced to flesh, to parts of the body, to the hunger that we trick ourselves into believing will be one day satiated. Eros is a relic of antiquity, on display in museums next to literature, art, and love letters. Hermes, brutalized by information technology, has flung himself on Eros. *You are just one click away from a virtual brothel.*

A risqué utterance is electrifying during sex. But foul language debases me, the swagger and braggadocio of a nation once host of the Etruscan Atlantis and today avant-garde of inanity. It humiliates me, the defensive reduction of Eros to the common sense of the common man. It's cowardice, to interpret the passion and enthusiasm of a male who is no longer young to the potential acquisition of *fresh pussy*. I hate the phony wisdom of the man of the street. The common man is racist, colonialist, fascist, Mussolinian, Berlusconian. It mystifies me, the squalid vulgarity I had naively misread as post-feminist irony. I cannot forgive myself for having thought that the exploits of a handful of seekers of knowledge could influence the sentiments of an entire epoch. The idea that the students' and workers' revolt of the nineteen-sixties and -seventies could have unwittingly laid the foundations of our squalid present gives me sleepless nights. Our present era lives transgression as a fashionable gesture sponsored by the corporations, and the once groundbreaking motto *nothing is true, everything is permitted*, has become the jingle of global capitalism.

Our street embraces and protests were animated by a sense of justice, hence of ethics. It humiliates me, seeing the daily fascism and the blind vitalism rearing its head in lovers' bedrooms, right into the dark sacredness of sex and love.

Already the boudoir is stuffed with trophies and skulls of past loves. Already a congregation of brand new skeletons crowds the courtyard waiting to join the grand finale, the naked dance on the deathbed when pleasure given & pleasure received turn out to be the anxious gesticulations of baffled souls who lost their core on a distant day and never found it again, never ever found it again. Already we hear the jarring chords of a Requiem played by an orchestra of debutantes. A slow drowsiness seizes us (*God, if only I could sleep for a few minutes*), a metaphysical drowsiness, the very drowsiness of metaphysics, the heaviness of this flight of futile consolation above our sad affairs.

* * *

Did I just doze off? Don't know. I refuse to look at the clock. I would gladly swap my PhD. erudition Piled High and Deep like shit through the years for a good hour of sleep that would restore me to the metaphysical illusion, to the superficiality of sleepers and metaphysicians. There's superficiality and super-ficiality: 1) There is the superficiality of those who imagine that depth must exist somewhere, the amalgam perhaps of various notions reified by poetic doodling sketched on water through the centuries: *God, the Unconscious, Buddha-nature, History, Dialectical Materialism, the Actualizing Tendency, Europe, Being, Truth.* 2) Then there is the superficiality *ad litteram* of those who have woken up (with no fanfare, without the special effects of so called spiritual enlightenment) to the realization that there is no hidden coming-and-going behind the stage curtain (no being behind becoming; no sublime behind the everyday; no absolute behind the relative), and are able to embrace what is as it presents itself to the alert senses. Profound is after all only that which is remote: darkness for the eye, silence for the ear, non-being for being. The former speak of 'peak experiences': they fall in love right, left and centre, break their neck or prostrate themselves at the altar of a god never seen to be defecating, a god considered such because one has not seen it defecate. They flee the everyday, hastily construed as banal, a realm in which work is equal to punishment.

From Nietzsche (genius of suffering), Valéry (genius of despair) and Proust (genius of jealousy) one learns not so much the inevitability of affliction as the possibility of extracting raw diamonds from it. This type of learning is foreign to the Judaeo-Christian perspective. It belongs to the existential perspective, on a good day.

In the realm of love we pay a high price for escaping from the inevitable disappointment and a broken heart. We pay via dissociation and the selling out of our very humanity. Farewells are an example of this. A person in love experiences departure and separation as mourning, albeit momentarily.

The stronger the love, the more acute the perception is of the transient nature of existence. (Before the sweetness of melancholy overwhelms me, Melanie Klein soberly reminds me of the opposite pole of the equation: the stronger the *hatred* of the loved one, the deeper the sadness in parting, linked as it is to the desire to destroy the one who, having so much power over my feelings, makes me suffer). In the attempt to avoid our slipping into victim mode, we miss the incommensurable gift of vulnerability.

I was coming back from work; it was pouring with rain and there was a cold wind. Sheltered under the bus stop I looked at the rain. Then, I don't know how, the anguish and despair I felt turned into inexpressible joy... It is not possible to force such moments of rapture, when the fragile beauty of the world is revealed to us. Maybe these intermittences of the heart are but small trophies, and yet in recounting such cheerful shipwreck I know that I'll miss its consolatory music on this endless night.

* * *

I speak to you from a place beyond the grave, from an autumn I do not recognize in spite of the stubborn grace by which the tree opposite my house reproduces its motions, in spite of John Keat's pagan *puer* asleep in the hay. The summer that went past was life, and summer is over. I whisper this from a sleepless night, and insomnia is for me a gift: I refuse to swallow sleeping pills, or sign up for a cognitive-behavioural treatment. Insomnia is my metaphysical revolt, an act of *resistance*, my own personal refusal to lean on anything; to the life of a happy primate, of a reconstructed chimpanzee leaning on the soft pillows of a new belief system I prefer the human wound ablaze in the hour of no healing.

* * *

I have loved the sea since childhood, since the day my mother taught me how to swim. I'd imitate her and go far and felt blessed with water and sky, happy to exist. I loved the sea in Calabria, and during a journey from Brindisi to Athens, learning by heart and on an empty stomach Rimbaud's *Illuminations*. I loved the Indian Ocean, its grey ferocity at the end of the monsoon season glimpsed by a convalescent bed, tended by a Dutch love (where are you now, M.? did you forgive me for having left? A shudder darts through me when I think of you on this endless night. I see your smile our morning hours stretched out on a nineteenth-century balcony, the exultation of protracted pleasure. I loved the ocean from a house on a cliff in California, resting at sunset after twelve hours of labour (where are you now, S.?).

I love the sea, even the puddle of Italic shores... I dozed off and dreamt of us two after a swim among the rocks (the tenderness I felt in seeing you in my dream tentatively entering the water) and from a screen up on the wall MTV played Carly Simon's *Coming around again* prophetic words in the refrain *there is so much room in a broken heart...* But you can't fool around with the sea: I had sensed in your sea imagery the impersonality that later on flooded the bridge I hopelessly tried to build. The sea is dissolution and oblivion; from its reflections we weave the infatuations and longings of earthly life. Andrei Tarkovsky knew about this and expressed it beautifully in *Solaris*. Joseph Conrad too knew that you don't, no you don't fool around with the sea. No thanks, I belong to *terra firma*, to the heat of lovers – to the newborn's ancient face, to the pain of mothers (but what do I know?). I belong to the earth. No one walked on water. Isn't there enough beauty and grace when you walk on earth?

Of course I love the sea, but in the sea the miracle of individuality is dissolved. Tin-can mysticism and wisdom-while-u-wait are not for me, I'm afraid: I've lived too long in these barren regions. I have been the lighthouse guard, happy to finger each constellation in turn, contented to breathe in and exhale my own private ecstasies. Dispensed busloads of platitudes; covered my cracks with a hand of fresh paint. After forty years I found that 'working on oneself' is but a descent into the abyss. An abyss of light: Nietzsche's impossible image confounds me and gives me solace in this endless night. Fritz (*Joyful Science, V, 343*) spoke of the open sea, of new dangers and new fears that seekers of knowledge and true sailors must face. On reflection, though, the sailor clings to the linear perspicacity of a daily routine that on a ship keeps at bay the tedium of water and sky; connoisseur of every brothel and tavern on land, paradises where every woman is a tender-hearted whore and every host a poet.

Angels & sailors, such fatal union seized me as a twenty-year-old on June nights (cursed month, month of Hermes and Aphrodite), inviting me to pull out of the bright sky the paths of ancient navigators, my fingers bloodied by the menstruation of a lover whose name and face are long forgotten (but not her dark sex, not her skin and the heady perfume, not her moans and sighs). I knew already it back then: it is my sex they want, not my poetry.

The sailor who ventures between water and clouds is not Ulysses hauling out the rudiments of his mercenary science from astral routes and quiescent monsters. Ulysses, scientific informer, wants to detain experience, convert it into knowledge but he doesn't know how to listen to the sirens' tune, doesn't know how to give in to their deadly song. They rest on him: the de-humanizing objectivity of science, the vainglory of technology and hubris of white medicine cabinets. He boasts of a mission, even a goal, raising knowledge to fetish status. It was not a scientist, the hero whose footprints lovers found at dawn among the seaweed, but a human being who, like the most revered among the Achaeans, was subject to lust and wrath, to the folly of the errant gaze, to the *inconsulta temeritas* condemned by prim Plato from the pulpit of presumptuous probity. Achilles stands alone among Homeric heroes in full recognition of his own mortality. He knows he is inferior to the gods for the mere fact of having been born. From here stems his disappointment with the war code, his profound solitude and the inconsolable sadness of his lyre. Not just his physical prowess, or the intellect, or the 'work on oneself'; not just the music and the poetry... Instead his vulnerability, the fall (brought about by Polyxena's betrayal), the unique beauty of the mortal hero, of the hero as a human being – so remote from the modern hero, the man-object of billboards, the shiny avatar of virtual worlds. In a nutshell: not Ulysses, but Hart Crane, who followed the sirens' song to the bitter end.

But I'm raving... I've had enough in fact of sea and sirens. And in any case a siren is not the muse but a run-of-the-mill chanteuse with a bloated face; an insecure, whorish creature who mistakes her cheap melodramas for love, who gulps up in her phony embraces credulous voyagers stranded and with their heart dangerously open, gambling their dear life for the bogus pleasures of a balmy night. They start believing that dreams will brim over into the light of day, that life itself might become poetry! And all just to escape the cruelty of the sea! A rude awakening awaits them, I tell you. When the effect of the potion starts to fade, they'll gasp like crabs thrown in the boiling pot.

II

Daybreak has to come at last, the dawn of the Day of the Dead, and with daybreak some common sense! Stones in the hall, the sun of my homeland: time before information technology, when human feelings had bright rooms to waltz in, widening circles to infinity, rhythm and sequence; time before swift hunger set in to bolt the other in clunky embrace. Inestimable value of distance – allowing silence to weave ever-new and unknown patterns. If only we could allow time for sketches of *Moira* who is higher than the gods. Finally the cells mend themselves without fuss: praise to the incomplete, to what is eternally suspended.

* * *

Unforgivable blunder: tracing back one's steps, crossing the automatic barrier at stations or airports, begging the attendant to let you in, to make an exception. Orpheus' mistake: turning to look at Eurydice who vanishes and becomes a memory.

But is not memory herself the real Muse, the one addressee worthy of love? Is not Mnemosyne herself imagination and poetry, the locus where the soul of the world absent-mindedly grazes, in perpetual exile, serene in the ecstasy of things undone? My one unforgivable blunder to which I owe the curse of impossible love.

Orpheus at central station just stands there, watching the train go, the train that takes her back to the land of the shadows. I failed to reply – how could I? – to your double request: a) unsheathe the sword, having dismounted, and tear you away from the spasmodic embrace of your tribe; b) enter your world on tiptoe, wed it without altering it in, become a pattern in the wallpaper. Unforgivable blunder: cultivating heartache after farewells, anemones in the garden of sorrow fertilized by distance. A fatal blunder in our technological era that seals the end of literature, the end of Eros, the end of sumptuous pleasure extracted like honey from the petals of defeat – antechamber of happiness – from the inevitable defeats of love.

The end of *a madness most discreet*; the end of *my only love sprung from my only hate!* And it's not just Shakespeare reiterating this via his Veronese dabblers, but also the Shakespearean novelist Sigmund Freud. For hatred is more ancient than love. Our instincts would thrust us into a tragic scenario but technology saves us for pleasant mediocrity, but even in non-virtual life one can escape the chaos of relating by turning every lover into an illustration, a signpost, a stage in a path unscathed by contact. A gloriously sterile path: welcome to the tourism of relationships and the virtual safari. Don Juan knew it well, and every man or woman for whom encounter is a step in a pointless journey, unmoved by sorrow or joy. Is it narcissism? But to bequeath this clinical slur to emotional sightseeing is an insult to Narcissus to whom we owe the precious little we know about the self. No, we are still in the playground of seduction, and seduction is, in a wide sense, sublimation. *Se-ducere* is to take oneself (or another) away from one's real path: distraction, deviation, and detour. Is this the set course for contemporary women: from seduced seductresses to independent mothers? No, this is not the province of Narcissus, for the sixteen-year-old boy is tormented by a passion for a mirage.

The hyperboles of love: at the death of Antonio, Cleopatra said: *there is nothing left remarkable under the visiting moon.* If it was not for love and love's hyperboles, what would we utter when out of breath, through whispers and broken words and caresses… A dog bark in the distant valley, then the sound of cicadas: *life is cruel, cruel, cruel*...We could fly into the distance and right into a Chagall painting. We understand every sound and enter phenomena, fired by a lyricism that inflames us. And finally sets us apart.

Not that the everyday becomes grey; rather, each new enthusiasm renews *ordination* – not to liturgy and beliefs, or the Dharma of incense and statues, but ordination into living-and-dying, *ordination to praise* – from Kandinsky's geometries to the symmetries of supermarket shelves.

* * *

What is it? I don't know. Most people call it love – the longing, the sweet pain, reckless smile breaking through a countenance at rush hour, the silence descending in the midst of city noise. To inhabit such distance is the consolation of memory, the certainty of defeat in days that start to fade and give way to autumn. Sitting in my room in the late afternoon I feel the sun and life itself on the planet dissolving. In the vast silence I mourn the momentary absence of pain. Re-entering this flighty skin, I embrace again my destiny after the detour of seduction. Is this path the very path of erotic thought? Seduced by love, we are prey to hatred, for hatred is far more ancient. Unable to resist the vicissitudes of the instincts reawakened by touch, we run for shelter to priestly blessings, to a thalamus that may keep the Furies at bay. Others flee: they run as fast as they can from the inevitability of hatred; they rummage in the crowd looking for short-term tenderness and frantic embraces. The deed is done, and half asleep they search for a melody among the sheets and in the first sound of dawn. Unmovable, untouched, they pursue their reticent, introverted path. Rotten luck of contemporary woman, offspring of feminism: once seduced seductress, now 'independent mother'. They dart past you, these young mothers, from a yoga weekend to a ceramic workshop, bad poetry and shopping lists in their head, perched between hints of tenderness and the episodic groans of a life implied. And ye shall faithfully trail the stream of seduction, for seduction is sublimation. And embers will bear witness to the fatuous flame of summer. Some cut it short, take their leave early on: I envy them. Others linger on, divining embers and remains on sleepless nights, simmering sense and direction.

* * *

Many have said it: you go back to your native land and find it changed. So you become a stranger in your homeland. You travelled from A to B. In going back, you discover A has become C. Unrecognizable. Shopping malls where once there was open space.

I left Italy in 1984. I travelled for six years – lived in France, Germany, India, and the United States. In 1990 London became my home. The city welcomed me as it welcomed from time immemorial exiles, refugees, and émigrés from the colonies of the Empire. 'Londoner' is to this day synonym and symptom of ambivalence – wobbly sense of belonging, an absence of roots. The interlocutor hesitates: Londoner? It can mean all and nothing. He waits, is tentative. After a while the accent, a gesture, the way a person walks reveal the shade of a belonging, but what is revealed is a remnant that sheds its hue as we speak. Who leaves the homeland becomes a hybrid: not entirely English, no longer Italian: a monster. This could create pain, if belonging to a tribe were important to me, but the thing is, being uprooted suits me just fine, thank you very much, for I am one of those who sing on their way to the gallows. Stateless, and childless too. In love with love beyond the preservation of the species. Devoted to ecstatic consummation, paying back the munificence and grace bestowed on me from birth. My private credo: praise the fragile beauty of the dew, do not attempt to organize goodness, for ethics are but generous folly. Power of the lotus flower and of the rose, stronger than the stone. The experience of the limit. I had tears of gratitude when someone reminded me of Lama Yeshe. Long before my 'nihilist' writings made me persona non grata in the Institute for the Embalming of the Teachings of the Great Vehicle. Finally, a pagan archangel resurrecting in me the accident called grace, annunciation in the midst of the traffic jam where I exercise my duties as citizen of the world, loyal to the carousel of alienation.

How I had loathed the *Bel Paese* with its crooks as Prime Ministers and its dapper scroungers, with rockers sponsored by corporations and murderers clearing their throat in ostentatious humility before singing in church. But the so-called homeland has touched my heart. What virtuous deeds did I perform, I thought, to deserve such bliss? What test awaits yours truly? So much joy is unsustainable. The past – luminous, transfigured – was knock-knock-knocking at my door, beckoning me in. It became present: joyful, ecstatic, yet modest in its grandeur. I asked myself: where from here? The path is lost in the wood and footprints fade. Under the open sky, all directions are possible, a troubled freedom, chance in ambush at every corner. In disclaiming linear time, every minute is apocalypse and the liberation following the refusal of a bargained redemption. In disclaiming dialectical encounter, the chance of poetry arises, the recognition of the other's unknowability. The abyss between the two shores is not filled, explained away or hidden. We decline from building bridges, from seducing and convincing. We swim together in the pond where a heron elegantly skims as we speak.

* * *

I accept your accusation of *narcissism*. I salute the *new madness* sung by Ovid. Welcoming the insult, I face up to inner tumult and bow to you, virtual lover in a dream that once was and now is no more. To the evocative sound of your voice, Echo, Narcissus bows, o nymph who waited on a summer day by the prayer wheel, bequeathing a semblance of *logos* to your recurring *melos*, giving life to phrases heard in the antechamber of dreams. From the beginning I, Narcissus, loved in you a mirage. From the beginning I loved in you the remoteness of provincial life, that intimacy unknown to my Babylonian solitude.

Thanks to me, Narcissus, the soul can evict exterior deities generating for the first time interiority. To me, Narcissus, all of you folks owe the very birth of inner life, linked (sure, like the river to the sea etc.) to the *anima mundi*. Yet without the ford in the river (*drunken boat* as well as *heart of darkness*) to approach the sea is certain shipwreck. Soul (*psyche*) is born with me, Narcissus. All of you lot owe it to me, your imaginary distance from Darwinian monkeys. It's not my fault or is it? If the Judeo-Christian brigades have later regimented the soul, frozen it inside a monad, preserved in formaldehyde until judgment day. If I, Narcissus, am allowed to live (but usually you all want me dead in tender youth, as Icarus, as Hart Crane, as Jeff Buckley whose songs you forgot already, as Luigi Tenco whose songs never win a prize at Sanremo), I will then one day reveal myself to be the wise hermit of the fables. Same applies to Rimbaud, who would have surely become Imam or Benedictine mystic at the age of seventy-two if he had been allowed another go at the Russian roulette.

From the folly of interiority naturally we cross to the horizontal serenity of phenomena; *Tathata*, in the words of the old swindler Buddha Shakyamuni; being-in-the-world, according to the highfaluting tones of that renowned *Schwartzwald* redneck.

Onto this shore we disembark at last via the waterways of interiority (a journey that is painful, ecstatic and finally grotesque), harder to perceive in the epoch of bad infinity and information technology. Narcissism? If only we were given the chance to linger in the ruinous arcadia of Echo and Narcissus! If only we had access to the privilege of metamorphosis – of Narcissus into a flower, of Echo in disincarnate voice!

The self-combustion that in these beings produces a metamorphosis is fostered by the passions to which they abandon themselves, thus honouring human emotions and passions (consider this: even the gods give in to them). On the other hand, the 'narcissism' of a virtual avatar is the part-time, half-hearted metamorphosis of a bored and frustrated individual seeking with such egoic fantasies to flee both passions and emotions, to flee what Nietzsche called the 'magnificent monsters'.

The magnificent monsters are the true protagonists of Ovid's *Metamorphoses*. Violent, unpredictable, overwhelming passions perturbing the self and fraying the fragile membrane of an armour. Passions educate the self, make it humble, more malleable (if it survives the threat of a flooding of the unconscious into psychosis), more willing to honour their presence. Passions are part of the vast psychic territory which the ego must respectfully take into consideration. In dreams too, in spite of the interpretative recipes and their utilitarian function in aid of 'health, wealth and love', the ego must genuflect and watch their plot unravel in the theatre of memory, perceiving itself as one among many spectators of a drama. A virtual avatar is instead a phantom of the ego, the synthetic creation of an entity nailed to a computer screen. Not sub-personality, but fabrication, projection of one's own frustrated will to power. Not a journey through Hades or the vast ocean of the soul but reproduction and multiplication of a double repeating litanies along a sterile path. With the fake liberty of a virtual avatar the Platonic delirium of transcendence is finally actualized – escape from corporality, the arrogance of having understood and assimilated the body, forgetting that the body is a mystery.

An avatar does not sweat, does not come. He is immune to the emotional and subtle current and the sub-currents emanating from human bodies. The virtual avatar, as well as the spiritual avatar, are at the opposite pole from the Nietzschean overman and of the person of the Dao. To shun love's wounds one gives in to the acrobatics of a Don Juan (except that Mozart's *ouverture* begins, like philosophy itself, with a minor chord) and I wonder if it's only men resorting to such poor expedient. Each partner becomes symbol and bookmark along an isolated track (in spite of tentacles and protuberances, in spite of pleasure's cavities inviting contact). The partner met (or rather bumped into) is dismissed once their function is used up. In such Don-Juanism of experience the 'desire' the other believes they are feeling for us never makes of us real objects of relation, i.e. autonomous persons endowed with sovereign humanity and experience. After decades of feminism we are back to the old models. Women want the strong protective male; but even the best men shiver in winter and it's the best men who are not afraid of vulnerability. The tallest tree feels the storm first and is the first to fall. Evolutionism is subverted. In the Darwinian order of things, adaptation happens thanks to the gross attributes of strength, shrewdness and cunning, but the intelligence of the overman, of the man of the Dao is not unlike the fragility of a flower and the elusive magic of the dew. No more the authenticity smuggled by Heidegger, no more the umbilical link to the abstraction of the neutral Being, but instead vulnerability as new criterion of integrity.

Are you shy or are you pretending? I *am* shy, I am dumb when faced with the magnificence of living-and-dying, with the power of love, with the pagan sanctity of affirming this existence in which we are thrown (like an actor on a stage who has forgotten his lines, like a rain dog) and at the same time overwhelmed by a shower of cherry blossoms.

The first is the classic stance of the philosophy of existence. The second is the response of grace, gratuitous sovereign in moments of genuine forgiveness, of love saved from atavistic hatred, grace hidden in the everyday, visible to the initiates, to Kierkegaard's Knight of Faith, to the soldier who comes back from the Crusades disenchanted and alone and who during a pause in the game of chess with death praises the beauty of the passing moment and the strawberries offered to him by traveling artists.

I love Carl Rogers' vulnerability, the imperfect humanity transpiring from his life before his teaching ever became a new canon. His sleepless nights, the affairs, the use of alcohol in the last years of his life... Rogers emerges as a human being, contradictory and vulnerable. Authenticity, especially in a man, must be apprehended as openness and willing exposure to the uncertainties of existence. At the same time, this cannot be allowed to subside again into the male weakness of the nineteen-eighties, with its literal interpretation of the Jungian *anima* and of the feminine principle, which along with various other factors contributed to the dwindling of many male fellow travellers, abandoning them to the mercy of mothers, wives and lovers, converting them into submissive beings, ethereal and emasculated. And yet 'post-feminism' is indistinguishable from the old models in our contemporary landscape of bad infinity (of proliferations of meanings, within the confusion of values as values *given* and not created).

A man in tears is an intolerable sight to some women. Perhaps they see again in a flashback their own father – until that moment considered omnipotent – pushed around by chaos and the waves of existence. Holding an image of ego's solidity (coveted, never achieved) is at the centre of many forms of anguish and dominates the sphere of fantasy, imagination and dreams. Dreams are significant because they debunk the solidity of the self. The *I* of a dream cannot be reduced to 'me'. Memory and imagination operate in a similar fashion. Poetry feeds on remoteness, flowers in the soul's landscape. Distant lovers (in forbidden or unconsummated love, the love curtailed by circumstances, by the inclemency of need and the triumph of the reality principle) feed on distance. Fantasy is instead egoic projection, distorted sense of superiority – related to the cowardice of lowlifes (nowadays adopted by global capitalism): on the ashes of identity, manufacturing an omnipotent image of oneself. This is also the foolish aspiration of cyber-avatars in the desert of the virtual worlds.

In the Hindu tradition an *avatar* is a realized being that descends into life as human in order to help others, a being who chooses the prison of the body/mind to communicate the good news: there *is* a vaster space, free and open, although at present this might be obscured by ignorance. The avatar is a messenger of an existence (fathomed as permanent) which is beyond *samsara*; an enlightened being who succeeded in evading impermanence. The cybernetic avatar is at the opposite pole: a projection of an omnipotent ego, born out of low self-esteem, out of resentment towards one's own human frailty, out of the terror towards the unpredictability of existence.

Both avatars, spiritual and cybernetic, are expressions of our desperate attempt to escape this valley of tears. Both are manifestations of human rancour towards the imperfection of becoming; both are marionettes modelled in the squalid workshop of resentment.

While the spiritual avatar has failed in his millennial mission of denigrating life and obliterating the body via various religious systems, the cybernetic avatar is for the time being succeeding. The avatar roaming virtual worlds exercises some degree of control, steering well clear of the sweat, blood and tears (but also of laughter and tragic joy), avoiding the nuts and bolts of the human condition, those attributes without which we cannot call ourselves human. We are more than ready to subjugate ourselves to something bigger, to make a deal with any deity and trade our devotion with the hope to be exempted from the dark night of the soul (or the death of God, or the great existential doubt). This so-called surrender employs sooner or later the features of authoritarian sadomasochism. The yoke could be an external deity or the divinity of one's own ego. Take your pick, don't be shy: both are made up. With the virtual avatar, 'absolute freedom' becomes in no time slavery to the idiocy of false needs and false desires. Angelic speed teleports us right into the demonic miasma of a promised land. We are the honoured guests inside the solipsistic cage, the VIPs in the mousetrap of subjective mysticism where every desire is granted, where objectivity (a state of mind of openness to the world) is drowned by the triumph of our most pathetic delusions.

* * *

Psyche catches Love in an alcove; she finds him barely awake and modest, gentle in his humanity and forgetful of his wings. Both are absorbed by the slowness that is the joy of the human dimension; both are ushered, plowing up the grayness of linear time, into the human realm of poetry. Angels envy us, they covet our inclinations, alien to them for these are distillation of suffering and precariousness. Angels only know speed, the immediacy that in their flight burns what is a mirage – our only reality – in the murky interlude between birth and death. Angels only know lightness and the ecstasy of reflected light.

Of all angels we love the fallen ones best; we love their rebellion and erotic intensity. Finding both attributes in the same fallen angel (as in Milton's splendid Satan) we bow in deep reverence and join as accomplices in his heady subversion of the firmament and his voyeuristic contemplation of Eve's voluptuous curves.

The opposite movement, of emulation and human aspiration to the angelic dimension, is escapism, denigration and antithesis of the aesthetic dimension: the magic arts of Milarepa, riding a ray of sun, traveling between hemispheres; Jesus, changing water into wine. But I want to ask: Is water not miracle enough?

The human becomes angelic out of excess, as an *error*. Hart Crane, Arthur Rimbaud: to inhabit poetry in one body and one soul. The rest is banality, asinine braying motivated by best intentions. Think of the cutting irony, the difficult aestheticism of Oscar Wilde reduced by Roberto Benigni's magniloquent populism to flashy Sanremese homily in praise of the Italian vice of sentimentality.

The human remains human and runs into the angelic only via the self-combustion of passion and compassion. In any case angels are messengers, their services must be handled with caution. Worshiping their speed is idolatry. Angels are frightening creatures, the frisson of wings on the floor of the living room where I sit in my exhausted reverie would kill me. Among the six realms, the Buddha did not favor the realm of the gods but the human, the only one through which there can be liberation. An angel is condemned to the eternal apparition of a long-deceased God, to the insalubrious exhalations of the divine carcass, cursed by instant wisdom to the obliteration of distance and dignified solitude. But humans can extract

34

poetry from the ephemeral and mine diamonds from the iridescent mud of their tentative existence.

The indiscriminate use of information technology burns distance. It robs us of the gift of solitude where love comes into flower. It robs us of the gift of love where solitude comes into flower. You were the archangel of a pagan annunciation; the androgynous archangel who appears in a vision to Joseph in the Gospel according to Pasolini.

* * *

And even now that your text messages sound like press releases from the Ministry of Health and Education, I feel nothing but tenderness for you. *How are you?* – you write in response to my suggestion to speak with an open heart – *here everything flows and I'm fine.* How am I? The tree in the garden is now bare and in the morning airplanes flying south above my balcony vanish inside autumn clouds. There might be solace in the easy art of indifference, a sense of satisfaction gained by one's momentary control over the magnificent monsters. A sad victory, for the price we pay for it is high: our very humanity quits, and once the heart is fenced we are shut to the world. There are other ways to distance oneself from the magnificent monsters: cynicism, for instance, or crudity. There are ways to exhibit one's superiority over the numen of sex, many ways to keep at bay the joy of the senses alight, many proficient ways to feign detachment from psyche, the multicoloured butterfly. We can raid its garden with ungainly steps, with our indiscretions and songs sang out of tune. Take the cruel hilarity of dirty jokes, where we snort and chuckle at the misfortune and inadequacy of some unlucky fellow; or the predisposition of the 'man of the street' (monster, racist, and colonialist) to conceive of squalid designs behind any noble and generous action. Consider then the claim that such vulgar unmasking coincides with the psychoanalytic method, with the stylish cynicism of Hobbes, with the pessimism of Schopenhauer and Freud, with the positivist devaluation operated by aristocratic minds such as Nietzsche's. But in Nietzsche we find freedom from vulgarity and cynicism, in him who courageously debunked the moral and religious pretense of our overrated species. The trans-valuation of all values did not lead him to crude cynicism, for he was able to cultivate veneration and respect for the inherent sacredness of passions.

Sex is a deity and if we want to make fun of it we must learn how to do it in a cautiously divine way, as celebrants of Dionysus. In his crudeness the average man (and the post-feminist woman who deludes herself by thinking of having re-appropriated a hypothetical ancestral femininity) betrays instead the laughter of Polonius. It betrays Newton's metallic compass in William Blake's painting; the scientist absorbed in his minute calculations and oblivious to the terrifying beauty all around...

Ministerial bulletins and dirty jokes exult in the snug superiority momentarily drawn between us and the magnificent monsters. *I'm fine, and you?* Everywhere the self wants to reassert its position within the landscape which instead belongs to psyche, multicoloured butterfly nailed to the table, dissected and now long-deceased. It is a declining civilization that can number among its aspirations being able to hear the death sigh of the multicoloured butterfly, psyche, exiled from the world, stabbed by cynicism, vulgarity and obscene language, its carcass desiccating in between the pages of ministerial bulletins, of your text messages, my ex-love, bloodless echoes of what once were love letters, your love letters, my ex-love.

Here it is then, the only sovereignty left to me: the melancholy of detachment, a sharp pain in my chest; to be preferred nevertheless to the vulgarity of setting up home in a place not my own, with two hamsters and a cat the colour of ashes, protected, or so one likes to think, from the abyss, from the hurricane quietly building up in the belly of the volcano in the land of your birth. Surely this is to be preferred to the hardening of the heart (but what if it turns out that love is the only event giving luster to existence?), of the atrophied heart, protected for fear of bleeding.

Like an assassin, a spectre, like a hungry ghost I walk the path near a lake, I reach a building dreamt up in my delirium and find the place deserted, asleep, shrouded in the lavish mist of memory. The soul is strengthened perhaps through memory, through dreams, in the crucible of pain where it swims around in circles, utterly lost.

The broken heart ceases to be a resting place, it expands in the autumn sky, in a dark archangel cloud marching steadily from the east, heralding a storm. The cracks in objects no longer let the light in, as auspicated by friendly theologies, but instead they declare desertion, to be filed under past event yet – and here is the tragedy – never assimilated. Not every event is experience. If we flutter from infatuation to disappointment to terror to rupture, we are ready for the circular repetition and the vicious circle. Future circumstances will be used to reattempt solution or completion. Here is another option: to assimilate an event as would an apprentice of love who has given, received and managed to maintain a tender heart, respect for the lover whom the adverse fortune has now cast as opponent in the cruel game of survival. In spite of the similarity, there is a difference between the compulsion to repeat and the experience of the eternal recurrence. The final test: to be ready to repeat the whole experience – the good bits and the awful ones – *eternally.*

* * *

And who should come to mind but Emma Bovary with her cheap sentimentality, the bad poetry of her gestures... Oh but the snow shall fall at last and kindly stupor will be my companion. I must freeze the heart; I must not feel anymore. I must become non-human. Tunnel of frost, catwalk where Ice Queens prance about: where does chilliness originate? Defence/ fear/ wound? On this interminable night I reflect on the two souls inhabiting the Italian psyche, the Etruscan and the Roman; aesthetic sensibility and braggadocio... But I have a headache, I don't trust what I'm saying, not a tiny bit. I am raving... Here it is, I've got it: there is rage behind the aloofness of your texts. It is rage coming out of my own lips. *Italians? The most illiterate people with the most ignorant ruling class*, says Pasolini via his alter ego Orson Wells in *La Ricotta*. And what to say of the province, dressed up, technological, sick with foulness and nonsense? What a letdown for Nietzsche who read excess of depth in Hellenic superficiality...

* * *

The original sin is the sin of property, and Adam was the first landowner, forerunner of petit bourgeois values now universal, kicked out of Eden by an agrarian deity.

Soul as *Polis*? Dear Plato, this town is in ruins, it suffered a blackout and every communication among its citizens has broken down. And in your utopia, surprise surprise, gypsies and exiles are kicked out of the walls of the sunny city. And if they come in sick to be cured, doctors report them to the police.

Soul as a firm? Dear Roshi, the capitalist confraternity suffered a major crash from Wall Street to the City, here in my lunar town of ghosts where the controller is drunk and wisdom is an avatar hired by Lunacy herself, a crazed avatar driven by profit and more profit, here where every landlord and landlady is a sadist.

Soul as the sea? Dear ex-love, but of course I love the sea, your brainless sea, the nauseating vastness that was my first love. The *adventure* of the sea, I hear you say. But what do we know of the tedium of the sailor's life, of the strenuous yearning to be buried in its depths?

* * *

The eerie calmness we reach once we know for certain that we are in hell... From *Café Chantant* to *Café Chagrin* is only a short step, intensity persists but implodes, it now feeds off one's own exhausted mind and who cares if it's night or day or if the wind howls in my reddened eyes. And no book, no matter how thoroughly I might search, contains my individual pain... *Where are you?* ... ... For a moment I saw you near me, with your cruelty gone... Where are the days and nights, hours spent on the angel's wings, fast and joyous in pursuing the infamy of history and correcting it with the tenderness of love? History reassembles itself now, restored to your celebrated *banality*, the greatest curse against life, against the life that is lavishly offered to us every moment. The everyday, with its peaks of cyber ecstasy and the sterile raptures of a Semiramis sitting crossed-legged in the lounge of a virtual bar in *second life*, an evil and lonesome spirit ruminating in a computerized pit, and me hanging head down from a rope forced to reconsider the vanity of my knowledge, the fragility of the slipknot tying me to existence. I summon up an empty platform, the train is about to depart on any Sunday, eternal, autumnal, drained by memory then rebuilt and ready to leave again in D minor just like philosophy, just like Mozart's *Don*

Juan.

I search the sky looking for the south – still? What south? Whose south? The south of what? From what latitude, longitude, according to what centre? The centre has dissolved, night is a deeper night and the only light is the reflected infernal spark of the grey river I love, (so many journeys not taken, i.e. a boat drunken with love on a heart of darkness along the dark river of Babylon from Charing Cross to Greenwich up and down along the barbaric river of my town, of the town I love). But there was no time, the river was going to the sea. There was no time, life had no time to lose, it ran breathless towards death, like this night of All Saints towards the Dawn of the Dead where the Furies wait for me with their make-up on, all dressed up for gory sunrise. The dead sleep off their tranquil deaths and I sit here wide awake with no anesthetic, with no religion or Platonism, without sex or love, without art or métier, without cyber avatar, without the religion of virtual reality, without the new consolation of Platonism for the people.

It is only a short step, let me say it, it's only a short step between the *Café Chantant* and the *Café Chagrin,* one moment is enough, getting used to the languor of the senses before the heart is torn from your breast by some ridiculous ice queen. Life? Bad poetry lived and loved in the Babel of voices of provincial Italy. The soul, I hear you say, the soul! The strokes of a clock in the kitchen of an eternal night; she finds shelter in sleep, he sits *zazen* all night to contemplate the beginning, with eyes half-closed contemplating the beginning, you hear me, the beginning of the end. Shadows in the infernal night of a lost eternal summer, the spent body of Passion, a distant church on a hill, a church desecrated by my presence. I see it now, the little church in the night of All Saints prelude to the bleeding Dawn of the Dead. Dark silhouettes huddle up all around it. I see your ancestors – they want you there, clutching the soil as a succulent plant, feeding on their bones on their memories and ancient fears, as a fat plant where on a summer day a butterfly landed by mistake (the error that moves the wheel of life and knowledge). I see an icon of the Virgin on top of the hill desecrated by my presence, where desperadoes go to pray. Mary, Kanzeon, Quan Yin, protector of wanderers in the vast and cold sea of existence in this night when clouds gather ominously, oh Avalokitesvara Bodhisattva, refuge of hellish beings, of sex-starved beings, of exiled poets and forlorn amazons, allow me, I pray, to have a taste of true solitude so that one day I may be able to truly love. Where, where is love? I have betrayed in my dreams my innocent companion for an Emma Bovary, for a *Soffocone* wine-taster who in turn betrayed me in the name of a generality: necessity, the everyday, second-rate realism, complementary to the sentimental enthusiasm that makes of her and of all of us, and without a glimmer of hope, Emma Bovaries (*oui, c'est moi*). *Marry me: I'll wait for you my whole life.* Mmh, Soffocone wine, let's see: it displays hints of vanilla, leather and dark chocolate; 90% Sangiovese, 7% Colorino, and 3% Canaiolo. Time of harvest: October; with velvety tannins, medium acidity and medium-long length on the palate, the wine is both approachable but structured and suitable to a variety of foods. *Marry me: I'll wait for you my whole life*

    5.30pm at the station; the vertiginous beauty of my city, every alley and street without you, and the angel of Baudelaire sleepy and unaware of the pain that breaks me, unaware of the train vanishing in the languid afternoon. Another day on the blue planet as the day when my mother died and I woke up unaware at dawn to listen to the gentle rain song on the pavement from a second-floor student cell, Freud's *Three Essays on Sexuality* on the tiny desk and the discovery, the discovery of hurried love, of out-of-breath love and ecstatic love right next to the discovery of death. And the train disappears and nobody leans out of the window to wave goodbye, that nobody is already busy communicating virtually with other nobodies in remote regions of the globe and this is how Eurydice vanishes, this is how Amor closes the eyelids of the initiates and sends them back to the realist dream of the provinces, to the narrow-mindedness of the soil, to the atavism of work-as-survival, to the atavism of holiday-as-despair.

I see it now, the church desecrated by my presence: it's a ship in a derelict harbour. Next to the icon of the Virgin there is a cage with a baby falcon. A stranger has opened the cage and after brief hesitation the bird has flown out, down in the valley and disappeared in the infernal night, away from the torment of this land where it stayed captive for a short season. Who clings to the soil is a prisoner for life and lives in between crinkled days and logical nights. He cannot but dream of dissolution and the ocean, dream the dream of every woman of the harbor, of every provincial man and woman bored to death and afraid to live outside a box of pastels. There is not much choice for Madame Bovary caught as she is between suffocation and the melodrama of annihilation. The fatal error: believing that intensity of feelings is depth, that hunger for sex is love, that despair makes one noble by design. I see it now, the church on the hill, the church desecrated by my presence. And I see, incongruously, the cemetery of a Calabrian night of my youth when my companions and I, drunk and in tears, went to shake its gates because we wanted to say farewell once again to a comrade killed and buried there a few days before.

I see a fire, the combustion will transform me into a yellow flower, Narcissus, into an angel or star of the summer nights, a star glimpsed from a car speeding through the Mediterranean summer, star of a day like any other, a star already dead and buried in the firmament, a star long forgotten. I am so thoroughly fed up with so much bad poetry. Twenty years in England cured me of melodrama and operetta. A menacing thunder brings me back to the present (but where, where is the present? show me), and no one near me in the eye of the storm to reassure me as in childhood days.

You must have thought of us sometimes, the beauty that shrouded us under the summer sky, how we succeeded in softening it without raiding its memory. Is not memory after all a faculty of the imagination, snapshots in the editing room assembling and disassembling aggregates at every season, reworking its meaning? Doesn't the past change with every single deed, altering its shape and flavour? In weak individuals burdened by the innumerable deaths, the final editing seals the memory in archetypal imprint, in a snapshot that will consign the event to ancestral archives. A brave soul will perhaps chew over blissful and unresolved material in the fluid sea of memory, without committing to a verdict. You must have thought of us, of our love under the ambiguous moonlight...before consigning the mystery to the glacial light of the hyper-real, to the theatre of the anecdote, to a milestone on Separation Highway. You must have revisited the musical notes that for an instant interrupted our ever-present rumina-tions. You must have thought of the ray infiltrating in the diving bell of the self, of the air and the scent of flowers we both felt inebriated by. Of how we fled – seeking shelter from such symphony and rapture of trees in bloom – alarmed when we saw that their roots dug deep inside the graves of innumerable deaths, dismayed in learning that *love* were only four letters written on water. So here we are then signing up for the waiting list of impossible loves, of hurried, half-consummated loves, a faded footnote in the tales of Eloise & Abelard, Pyramus & Thisbe, Echo & Narcissus... I had wanted your little life to overwhelm me, I had wanted to caress your solitude with my fingers and give you serenity with my timid love, with my strong love. My eyes are heavy, red with wakefulness. Women like you flee when they see a man's vulnerability, they interpret it as weakness; they flee from any real intimacy with a man. At first they cling with great intensity, hungry for love and caresses – a prelude to the Amazon flight in the wood, a run-up before the hasty return to the only sanctuary they know: the cave of the desolate heart, the solace of space where no one can reach them. I am thirsty... I sit in the dark cold kitchen sipping a glass of water. From so much pain something will have to be born, and I assure you it will not be my end. It is simply not allowed, in the world of troubadours and philosophers to which I belong, to let yourself be killed by a woman. Fritz composed his *Zarathustra* as alternative to suicide, and gold has been extracted from raw metals since time began. Who cares if my Muse is hellish and my song hoarse? I watch the thronged houses of sleepers in the suburbs, each one in his comfortable coffin before the dawn of judgment day. I watch the railing of the balcony and the poor plants neglected for a whole summer; I see the garden of love betrayed for a prolonged sip of Soffocone wine, with its well-known hints of vanilla, leather and dark chocolate. Time of harvest is October, Indian summer, the summer of the dead, of those weaned to the dark, of those who no longer hear the vain lament from these shores. Every autumn is a death rattle and how similar the wheeze of the dying to the moans of pleasure, how similar the moans of the dying to the love rattle.

I must have dozed off with my head dangling on the sofa...dreamt of tender and lighthearted love with a stranger, a French woman, fraught and fine-looking, an Emma Bovary who thought me an Arab, except that the I of the dream was not me. Then the time came to leave and I was at yours and you treated me with the affable indifference of one who replies to someone asking for directions at the station.

I would have loved you if you had been a stranger at the station. But the station was full of people, and I was there on the platform watching the train leave – no one leaning at the window, and the train went inexorably and vanished taking away Eurydice, unveiling the forgotten tragedy behind the Heraclitean *panta rei.*

How are you? Here everything flows and I'm fine. Everything flows towards death and oblivion. The Buddha turned the Dharma wheel, entered the stream of becoming – which is suffering, incessant change and death. And this state of things is in itself liberation. This is nirvana: the valley of tears and scrap metal where a train leaves eternally in your memory and tears away love from your very limbs and makes you lighter. This is liberation, awakening; this is so-called enlightenment: the unredeemable loss, the last stop of human doing. This is where the eminent cultivation of consciousness takes you, past the promise of happiness, sales talk of Buddhism: to an icy halleluiah, to the *lamma sabachtani,* to a heart fractured by the cruel beauty of a wounded dawn.

I look in the mirror and see an ancestor, an adventurer without scruples. I look in the mirror and see an arms trader and a slave merchant. I look in the mirror and find it empty. I no longer see a face of flesh subject to decay, nor the odourless and shiny avatar of the cyber rabble.

III

I wrote love poems once – sincere hence mediocre verses polluting the glacial joy with the *tralalà* of a broken heart. A weird detached happiness reigns when we obscurely understand that the apocalypse is within each breathing every moment, present yet without a trace. Passion embalmed by memory evaporates. Reason's cold daybreak unveils the cracks of infatuation. Sedated aggression, vanity, the sentimentality we hoped would resurrect us from dullness; the atrophied piano at the end of the room among plastic plants glistening with eternal and perfected love, a piano silently moaning in the nights of the black moon. *Ah my poor piano!* Emma Bovary exclaims. The piano, hushed, atrophied like a part of her, that same itch that makes us doubt that we are truly loved and shuts the heart in a snow cave. We heard remote, discordant notes between a practical deed and a necessary word in the liturgy of survival; a missed opportunity: it was meant to let a melody break out of the tired procession of hours and days. Alas poor Emerson! To no avail in your defiant godly ministry you speak of the divine passion of love! The naked bodies of men and women are but relics, replaced by the hungry fantasy of the flesh, married to the bloodless frenzy of omnipotence of virtual avatars. To no avail you spur us into welcoming the inevitable disappointments in love as balm that would make it more human. Already we run away, after our first night of tears, to complain to customer service and demand a new shiny item from the shelves. But what an old chestnut our futuristic race towards the ideal truly is, in hundreds of chat rooms and lonely hearts columns, in the antechambers of skype and *second life* where ominous desolation reverberates as from churches in ruins, abandoned by the God who used to reside there in the tragic era before the birth of the ideal. To no avail my dear Emerson you spur in us the detachment that follows genuine passion and transforms love into solidarity. Our 'detachment' is the scrap thrown away by disgruntled customers; our 'non-attachment' is dissociation from the affects, dressed up in Buddhist garments. We cannot stand the sight of broken idols, the maimed statues of Venus and Apollo, even though their beauty might consist in their fragility. The unmotivated beauty of the dew beautifies our mornings and vanishes with the first sunrays. The pointlessness of flowers makes life livable. Impossible to give a present that will not be weighed in the scales of resentment, and the sovereignty of the beginning feels now so remote! Once upon a time we struggled to find the words; what we do have words for is already dead in our heart. And I clung on to tiresome pranks trying to postpone the fall, wanting to give myself without restraint, all dressed in white in the black Mediterranean night.

Virtual sex and the meeting of avatars in the antechamber of *second life* are not mutation and metamorphosis. If they were, we should agree with Samuel Butler and say that the advent of technology implies the annihilation or at least the apocalyptically serene overcoming of the human dimension. Instead, virtual worlds are strictly guided by the most artless human idealism. They represent a return to the grand narratives post-modernism had naively believed defunct, including the time-honoured denigration of the human and of the body. But the human body (not the raw body of biology and atomism) remains a secret, it continues to astonish, as well as provoke horror and disgust. Bedfellow of death, at once walking corpse, etheric and erotic vibration: from the body we avert our gaze and turn towards the Platonic city from which the complexity of becoming is averted. The cult of cybernetics professes a devotion to horizontality but in fact rejoices in low-cost Platonism, the triumph of the idea outside and above the chaos of becoming. The avatar is a fake metamorphosis, a shortcut that allows us to flee the body (house in flames, anachronistic temple of ruins bearing witness to being human in the next future). I do not mourn the imaginary nemesis of the human but denounce instead the all-too-human plot guiding and manipulating each step of technology and cybernetics. I denounce the unresolved angst of the creature who dreams ethereal perfection, its gaze glued to a portable screen, its animal fingers clutching a mouse and a keyboard. I lay blame on the illusion of a trans-human future, and mourn the disbelief revered by Lyotard, the ironic incredulity in response to theologies and teleologies. With the advent of the cyber era and of the *strange guest at the door* (the nihilism of certainty), post-modern scepticism ends up representing the last glimpse of the human dream of intelligence.

Sweet twilight, the fragility of daybreak at Sils Maria and in London – if there will be a dawn at all after this interminable dark night... I do not mourn estrangement from humanity, nor reclaim an ephemeral membership to the vicissitudes of a species whose importance has been exaggerated and all too often narrated as epic tale – its pathetic journeys inside the celluloid of memory, on both sides of the stage curtain... I do not mourn the loss of the ego's vain dream – the melodrama of lovers, their ineffective balms. I sing instead the tragic joy of the twilight in a station empty of commuters at Kensal Rise where fascist-era loudspeakers declaim the vainglory of recorded timetables to crows and nettles. I sing the incomparable beauty of every dawn that always defies the stupidity of our species – millions of dawns untouched by the human dream of domination. To this non-human sphere plead the best minds of humanistic therapy, although they mostly dress their jargon with the requirements of etiquette and fully prostrated to the Zeitgeist. Carl Rogers' actualizing tendency is not the wish to actualize this fiction we call the self but affirms instead an impersonal will to power, or instinct of freedom, or life's desire to overcome itself. To such impersonality and even universality – and this is where transcendentalists of every persuasion fall flat on their venerable arse – one has access solely via *existing*, via bare living, what we take for granted and exploit as backdrop for the manufacturing of a phantom on whose neck we hang a label with our blessed name on it. But this phantom is but an assembly of aggregates (poorly perceived, badly studied) clumsily dragging along other assemblies of aggregates (poorly perceived, badly studied), gaze fixated on the horizon, forgetful of the humdrum splendour of the everyday, of the bare existence which is the very symphony of the spheres. In the meantime, outside the virtual screen the *folie a deux* unravels like an Ibsen drama or a Thomas Hardy novel: pierced by a ray of sun and not realizing that it soon will be night, lovers meet on the prettified and deadly ground of feelings. Choose among the following options: press 1 if you intend to drown in your feelings, for having failed to understand them; press 2 if you wish to collect another pearl for your necklace of pain, for yes, you *did* understand your feelings but have failed to acquire the means to assimilate them; and finally, dear customer, press 3 if what you really *really* want is to get lost in limbo, darling customer, considering that you have fully denied and denigrated the mighty power of feelings. Among such free choices, the third one will regale you with a sense of dignified belonging to schizoid normality, while the first two will give you the melancholy decorum of the human creature prostrated at the feet of the magnificent monsters. No matter the shape of our suffering and the exact nature of our stupidity, all this provides material aplenty for poets, philosophers and playwrights. For it is love that makes the world go round, and daybreak chases the night and on and on it goes.

And daybreak must surely come at last, the dawn of the Day of the Dead.

Hannah Arendt was eighteen when she became Heidegger's pupil at Marburg University in 1924. He was thirty-five. Three years later he would publish *Being and Time*. She was beautiful, he told her, and they became lovers; both genuflected at the altar of the genial mind of the philosopher. Heidegger publicly declared his support of the Nazis during the infamous talk in Freiburg in the spring of 1933. The summer of that year Arendt fled Germany and for seventeen years became an exile and a radical writer of high standing. In February 1950 she returned to Freiburg and in spite of the promise made to herself she phoned him from a hotel. The two lovers met and spent unforgettable days. Arendt later admitted in her letters that the only obstacle to her 'automatic' gesture of picking up the phone and dialing the number (the automatism of love, of gratuitous generosity) was not ideology, or history or destiny but *pride*. Pride prevents lovers after a long absence from saying *I love you my sweet one, I happen to be in your city, let's meet*. Love (tragic, immortal, yes, a love full of pathos) survives: *Eros, Amor, Liebe*, distant love, the distant sigh of a blue planet dissolved in ice, love full of pathos… what is life after all? The shadow of a fleeting dream. The brief fable is over, the true immortal is love.

If married to the liquid love of late capitalism, the non-attachment the spiritualist middle-classes prattle about offers a grand pretext for their inability to love. In such middling milieus two are essentially the pet hates: *attachment* and *projection*. But without attachment there is no relating, no *cathexis*, no leaning out of the diving bell of personality. And without projection there is no communication whatsoever, only a desolate echo inside a maze of mirrors. After their meeting, Heidegger wrote four letters in quick succession – sincere, passionate – to Hannah Arendt. He told her what joy her reappearance had brought into his life. A relationship of this kind would nowadays be judged harshly, filed in haste under transference and counter-transference. But Socrates and Plato knew it, and so did Freud and Oscar Wilde. Eros is the subterranean current between teacher and pupil, master and disciple, analyst and patient, and love is the burden we carry on our shoulders in the commuting journey from darkness to darkness, from light to abyss of light in this dark night. Classrooms are awash with erotic desire, with love unsaid and unconsummated between teachers and pupils. The stereotype demands the female pupil to be univocally exploited and then dismissed by an aged male tutor; it demands that pleasure be entirely his domain. Research and statistics show that, exposed to nubile Venusian bodies, the tutor suffers a contrast effect and perceives his older partner as less attractive which in turn would explain the high percentage of divorce among teachers etc. Schools are awash with the impetuosity of Eros and I don't believe you when you say that you would have loved me if you had caught a glimpse of me as a stranger in a station's waiting room. No, you loved what I represented; you loved the messenger. You raised me to the heavens and later tore down what you could not reach. Hannah Arendt picked up the phone after seventeen years. An irrational gesture, as with authentic forgiveness: unmotivated, or motivated by grace. Neither redemption, edification nor the crude fantasy of accomplished maturity, but the move of an angel, swift, preceding thought, preceding history as well as the birth, from the rugged womb of a *cogito*, of a separate I.

Attained at last: love spiritualized, love unworkable, o Alienor of Equitania! Truly I do not know if these vagaries of mine into your bosom thou shalt receive, o Madonna born in the shade of a volcano, or if you shall disparage them and the primeval pathos of an errant knight as un-developed and crass as I am, incapable of ataraxia, drowning in cheap brandy and cheaper nostalgia. Came to the reluctant conclusion (though momentary, empirical of course, awaiting ulterior verifications etc.) that we cannot ignore Doctor John Bowlby and his acute observations on attachment, loss and separation. We cannot ignore the etiology of affect and secure base. The detachment preceding and impeding the creation of an intimate relationship is as 'neurotic' as the blind yearning for symbiotic union. That symbiosis should come before disso-ciated separation confirms my thesis, gentlemen of the jury. So now answer me, Alienor, alien remote lover: can we truly depart from someone we haven't truly met? "And if love were but demonic intersection, the obscure flurry of blood and hormones?" the chorus of gravediggers ask in unison. And if love were mere dance of transference & counter-transference, raising its pathetic stems against the horizon only to mow them down to the music of a prosaic flute? And if the avatar were found to be master of the world, the technological overhuman conjured up by Herr Martin Heidegger? Is the avatar a John the Baptist or the Messiah himself of techno-logical transmutation of human nature and human deeds? The point of contention is not the alleged contamination by the machine, but the fact that such blatant anthropocentrism is being concealed by the seduction of virtual worlds.

Since the vicissitudes of Verona's amateurs, love has become an outlaw. *Where art thou Romeo*? Why, he is in a bar downtown, where else? He is sipping a semi-macchiato semi-skimmed medium frappuccino whilst sending clandestine text messages on his shiny mobile, accumulating erotic capital on *Fuckbook*, linked, linked-in, linked up. Love is contami-nated – impossible love exults all too briefly, transgressing the established order of things, painting secrets anew. The giddy rapture is always one step away from punishment in the orchard of the Capulets. I have a question: do Romeo and

Juliet enjoy more the fullness of being together or the thrill of being found out? The third party is an essential component if the criminal bliss of the illicit liaison is to continue. The ardour of the woman with her secret lover is being fuelled by revenge against her father. The man who betrays his companion flees from the image of a possessive mother. The scene is set for incumbent disaster, for the unwitting summon of the night mercifully bringing this preposterous suffering to an end.

So I found myself at the *Café Chagrin*, fully packed under a cold sky in an empty universe. I love your absence now that you are not here – power of love's negative theology. I chant an elegy to sunlight, to the absent God evoked by the notes of a mute symphony, soundtrack to the meeting of bodies who in mutual consummation enlarge the present time and fool each and everyone into believing that *this is love this is love this is love that I'm feeling*. Muzak of fake jazz now takes its place – we go back to our diving bells after a brief stroll on the bottom of the sea. *Dunno 'ow to 'andle this thing*. But I did warn you, didn't I, sweetie – what did I say? I said, *Beware, darling, I am just a poor devil*.

It humbles us somehow, having to bow down to the unbroken power of transference, dissociation and projection (first positive, then negative) of neglected or eclipsed parts of the self, even after decades of 'work on oneself'. Speaking of which, when will *working on oneself* come to an end and the celebration of our ephemeral life begin? Could it be that love *is* the work? And if we were to learn that this work (evolution, transformation, cosmetic art, you name it) is animated by our resentment towards impermanence, by the delirium of a metamorphosis deemed impossible, by the refusal to accept ourselves as human and transient, as no big fucking deal?

But why then do I find myself stupidly wanting to share with you, a mere fantasy, moments of joy like, say, the day before yesterday exiled from our virtual love all gathered inside my black coat telling a phantom in my head of a lovely morning spent with pupils studying the exhilarating journey of the soul undertaken by Jung? Why do I catch myself lost and happy in the blue icy noon while searching for a seat and then settling down to hot soup in a Chinese joint next to the theatre, why do I catch myself happy and exiled from love with the fixed gaze upon me of a blonde table-guest sharp as a fencing move? Precious little is allowed during lunch break – people gulp down their food, blather and laugh and cry and rub their hands in the blue ice of noon. Cut a long story short: still love you, kind of, only a bit less though, because of self-respect you know because of my innate sense of independence, of my dignity as a man for Chrissake. Yes I love you still, figment of my pseudo-emancipation, only a bit less though and under the morning shower hurrying along before work I improvise hate limericks, parodies of pop songs filled with insults where you come out all pummelled and buffeted, just what you deserve after all methinks ex- fake love of mine, considering that you have betrayed me for a bloody idea, a generality, as any fatuous creature straight out of Goddard, considering that you have betrayed me for your one true love, your stupid *pride*.

Hannah Arendt phoned Martin Heidegger after seventeen years and the meeting brought joy to both of them. An act of generosity, of folly, of gratuitous forgiveness, a.k.a. forgiveness motivated by grace. Now that I think of it, I wanted to sing the praise of triviality, against Heidegger's highfaluting redneck authenticity so popular in blooming existential psychotherapy... Instead I flounder about at the *Café Chagrin*, opposite the theatre, distracted by the cruel gossip of two pretty women seated at the table next to mine, one blonde one dark as the femmes fatale one meets at the crossroad of eternity, at the crossroad of destiny. Undecided between the two, our protagonist vanished into the cold street and went back to work.

Summing up: let the river follow its course; let it pass beyond the twenty-one days milestone; may the relics of a love that was be buried. Because *everything flows and I'm fine and how are you?* May familiar places re-assert their autonomous presence, free from the haphazard phantom of fantasy – station exits at Embankment and Belsize Park; Waterloo Bridge, the river, the dark river I survey every morning on my way to work. Because *everything flows* and all's well that ends well. Let winter follow autumn. May the year come to an end with a death rattle (and how similar the moan of the dying to the moans of pleasure). May new couples discover love and hatred anew in the immaculate dawn. May we all go happily back to work. May the everyday be splendid again. Because *everything flows*. And *I'm* doing just *fine*.

In the silence this night I hear the song of a sleepless bird, then another. A distant engine. Buried in sleep, my fellows roam the shadows of Hades. Wide awake, eyes wide open into the very heart of darkness, I lose the contours of things until the moon high in the sky restores the shapes that separate us. Everyone I'll meet in the morning will be the shadow of another; in his eyes I'll seek the code that might open me up to pervasive murmur. Providing there *will* be a morning, that the widespread glare I begin to perceive heralds its arrival and not the soiled radiations of a shameful end as written in the scriptures and in science-fiction cartoons. Provided another day will be granted, the Day of the Dead, so that I may take my debonair sorrow out for a stroll along the Camden canals, the enraged absence of your gaze in my gait, bearing witness to what everyone knows, that you can't give your life, you hear me, you just can't give your life to an Emma Bovary to some mixed-up individual who confuses intensity for 'grand emotions', who thinks she's given her heart when all she proffered was her body, who sips Soffocone wine believing it to be the wisdom elixir! Goldoni's innkeeper fancies herself as Lady Macbeth! You must be joking! And for what bloody reason, I ask in this night where even the moon is dark and hazy, why on earth should one get all stirred and genitally agitated if all this doesn't caress the soul? Why the exhausted tears and the sweat if from such tedious spluttering and expurgations we don't emerge with a heart more tender but with the armour intact, with the Heraclitean profanity of *everything flows* and *I'm doing just fine*?

Triumph of transference – as in Oscar's example, poor Oscar you understand, handcuffed in anno domini 1895, broken and cut in two, waiting for a train with two cops on a cold November day. Triumph of transference – as it occurred since Socrates and Plato – essential condition for the fertilization of knowledge, the subtle dance of Eros in ministerial classrooms. Triumph of transference – the sister with her hibernated heart eternally knocking at the door of conscience demanding the replay of our *folie a deux*. She comes back in disguise, dressed up as an Italian lover, assails you with the violence of amorous projection, chains you to a sofa after a sly embrace. Triumph of transference – the sister is younger prettier smarter; she appears as pupil on your course and says *I put you on a pedestal, I thought you were a great teacher, but now I think you are shit*. Triumph of counter-transference: come little sis, come and play with me. It makes me sad and it makes me mad when you refuse to play with me. Sister with a barricaded heart, a heart in the freezer while on TV they're showing *The da Vinci Code*.

The call of the homeland: biology, nostalgia, the alarming beauty of its hills, a whirl of emotions, the green eyes of a woman from Molise I believed to be dark, my perception clouded by twenty-four years in foreign lands. The price to pay if one obeys the call is one's own freedom. *Payul pangwa jangsem lag-len yin*: to abandon one's land is the practice of the bodhisattva. The immigrant lives a life in counterpoint, in two spatial and temporal dimensions at the same time, one receding in the background and refusing to vanish, giving out a perennially uncertain twilight glare, the other never fully becoming flesh and bone. After my final departure, the world has never been the same again; what linked me to it is forever broken. Homeland gods, tutelary deities and ancestors are now phantoms to me, hovering in the perennially uncertain glare of the dawn – inaccessible, anemic and remote. There is no greater solitude than the solitude of the immigrant. And if he finds himself in the liquid and exhilarating reality of a metropolis, he himself, like his own gods and ancestors, will become one of Baudelaire's wandering and homeless ghosts, an individual for whom no place can ever become, as once his native town was, the centre of the universe. His only hope is to make of the entire earth, of the whole blue planet his centre. There is no greater solitude than that of the cosmopolitan citizen. Homecoming? An illusion; you can never go back.

And if love itself were an illusion? Like Jacopo da Lentini, I am a ship broken by the sirens' smooth song. I naively believed the siren to be a muse. And what if the sceptical discipline of hope were an illusion too? We believed in gilded love, in the sunshine of an eternal June, but autumn follows summer and winter will be here soon, and death one day will come with two empty cavities where the eyes were and with bitter laugh, with an acrid taste in the mouth, as a door shut in one's face.

Not for me oh no the benevolence of a savior gesturing through the flames of love; if anything a drop, a lone drop distilled from the river of tears, a thin droplet of poetry. My own face emerges out of the dark well of insomnia: the face of *Farewell*, of *Too-late*, of *Nevermore*. *Unto thine ear I hold the dead seashell* and so forth. I extend my heartfelt thanks to Dante Gabriel Rossetti, equal partner in these hellish realms. The dead seashell brings to your ear ghostly whispers from a garden in summer – you dream of lovers reading haikus, slanted light in the darkness of the firmament, the darkness that claims me with its deadly whispers on this endless night. Couldn't have been otherwise. I find in my biography a continuum punctuating the silent triumph of negative theology: God is great because he is absent; the homeland is present because it's lost; love unreachable and finally trans-figured, taking its leave, becoming the longing for poetry, the longing *of* poetry, the song of distance, a thirst never quenched. How can I rely on the deranged logos of sleep-lessness? But isn't perhaps in this nudity, in this very wound an echo of our condition as refugees, of storytellers who lie down on a field at night and gaze at the sky and are suddenly startled by the mystery? With Kierkegaard, faith becomes dangerous. With the Romantics, love becomes risk-taking. Religion and love both restored to the straightforwardness of existential questions. I'm not speaking of a melodramatic faith that makes of every pain a *tralalà*, or of the pornographic rapture hiding a deadly incapacity to give. The nakedness of the body simply hides real nakedness, i.e. vulnerability, being open to caress, to the other's imperfections. In covert love, founded on passion and on the unreality of short-lived encounters where the blood reaches boiling point, the flame dances at first, and later solidifies in frenetic sex fuelled by desperation. It is then of course an act of courtesy to let a lover believe that sex with the spouse isn't quite as satisfying. Economizing with the truth is in such cases an act of tenderness. If love is to survive the flimsy glare of summer, lovers need to direct the flame into a common task. But the task is hijacked by generalities: matrimony, property, children, obeisance to conventions founded on the blind imperative of the continuation of the species. The creation of a *third* is essential: an offering, a hymn of praise to existence that allows the fortuitous and miraculous encounter: the locus of art, of meditation, of an ecstatic dance that respects natural distance.

You won, I admit it, and I know why: to my bad poetry you opposed the everyday, the very same weapon I had brandished in order to circumvent the pseudo-religious seductions of Heidegger (it was to be my personal tribute to Lefebvre, to Lukacs and to the now subterranean river of Heraclitus), to circumvent the pseudo-philosophical seductions of all religions. You managed to use the everyday (home, work, child and so forth) as a weapon brandished in the name of drab realism, right inside the domain of *das Man*, right inside universal quiet desperation. But it wasn't you who did the talking, oh no, now I know. It was the dark virgin in black, the creature who from time to time borrows your name to plaster the error of your ways, the sin of gratuitous happiness, to rectify through her raptures of contrition the primal error: being in the world without any bloody reason. The dark virgin is a nurse. The dark virgin is a scientific informer. She never quite kills what she loves but keeps it hanging between life and death. This is because her specialty – some say her addiction – is to perform artificial respiration.

How things truly are: the room of the natural health centre where I work has a clock on the wall opposite and an alarm clock next to the window. I sit here waiting for a client. Silence is absolute, enunciated by the sharp counterpoint ticking, one pursuing the other sometimes to contradict, sometimes to validate its claim. Linear time is death, legalizing the ineluctability of separation. Only love and desire are able to resist it. At first, a desire to touch and caress, a desire to take.

Then the desire to be taken, to become one with the beloved. Hermaphroditic fluctuations between polarities. Episodic union catapults lovers into deeper and more painful separations. John Berger tells us how in Caravaggio's *Narcissus* the face catches fire for a moment; it is a lamp lit in the darkness surrounding us, hanging over us. For a moment we tail the twinkle, the tenuous warmth of the apparition before going back to the shrouding darkness protecting us, like death, from having to *exist*, i.e., to come out, to *exit*. Desire alone makes us exist… Only desire makes us exit the ego's diving bell. Desire alone defies separation. But only brave souls know how to hold quixotic combat with entropy and gravity, with the double ticking of clock of the clinic where I sit waiting for a client who is late and has perhaps abandoned her contest with entropy and gravity, with the blind belief in linear time, in being-towards-death in which Heidegger, orphan of Arendt, wanted to believe. Could it be that bitterness against the fleeting nature of life is what animates the psychotherapy?

Against Time I'll use the shield Memory and the poetry of Desire. In the theatre of Memory your eyes will remain as they are (*what colour are they?*) and your lips will manage a smile. In the theatre of Memory which is the theatre of Hades you will remember my eyes, those eyes who once loved you. You'll also remember the shyness for which you used to mock me. In the theatre of Memory which is the theatre of shadows every embrace will recur eternally – question without an answer, *koan* unresolved, free from the servile obligation to perpetuate our spectral species. We defied original cruelty and our exiled steps now revisit its rocky path, aware of the body aflame, as a night star reveals to us as to Caravaggio our brief passage on the blue planet.

I love London: among its metal and dust I was born again in the spring of '89, stealing two narcissi from a suburban garden in Kilburn, and in January of 1990 I was baptized again on a bare floor in Cricklewood by someone who vanished leaving a trail of childish laughter. Love graffiti on the plane tree next to the tiny bridge that saw us ill-concealed with our breaths hung on unmovable time, inexorable yet clement time agreeing to carry us hand in hand for a while along the river (not the ocean, not the sea), along the dark river Thames. Heraclitus's river: dreamy, celebrating appearance.

How naïve to expect that the Western world would listen to Heraclitus rather than to that pair of buffoons Socrates/Plato! The world needs the grand scheme, doesn't know what to do with fragmentation. Even a gratuitous aimless act such as meditation is divulged and classified as 'tool' by the utilitarian brigades: selling water by the river. Meditation: useful for relaxation, good for health, to lower cholesterol; constructive to the creation of a new Platonic utopia, the Polis from whose walls (surprise surprise) fragmentation, incoherence, gratuitousness will be excluded (alongside refugees, homeless, and gypsies).

English melancholy has become congenial to me; the contemplation of dust, the *dustsceawung* of the ancient Saxons, those archetypal laments of wanderers and sailors, full of the exile's chagrin and loneliness. I *can* laugh and dance. But tonight I am not running away from melancholy, from this window open to the damp wealth of the soul, from the dark space that feeds on my sailor's face. Only those who did not travel long on it idealize the ocean, that lugubrious desert of water and sky. Only those who never left friends and loved ones on the shore, who did not open their eyes to the tragedy of impermanence can disport themselves with ocean metaphors. But in the ocean everything slips away and you find yourself alone, facing the *wyrd*, facing what will be, the disquieting fate sang by the ancient Anglo-Saxons. I wander among the ruins of ancient temples and realize that of all those works and deeds what remains are scattered fragments.

These very same words the dust covers them fast. You will read them in a remote corner and will perhaps remember a love, an all-too-distant love. It exists among Italians too, such contemplation of dust and I recognize it in disparate souls, from Foscolo to Tenco, and in the serenely meditative countenance of my friend Subhaga. Such aristocratic and humane spirit does exist under the braggart veneer inherited by the Caesars and by the daily fascism of the common man or woman who delights in inventing new versions of *Schadenfreude* under the shade of cypresses.

Unthinkable, in the era of information technology and of Big Brother, the diamond that is *Anatomy of Melancholy* by Robert Burton. We rely instead on anti-depressants, breathlessly we run to the nearest counsellor wanting to shed this sadness that is instead the dusty threshold of soul, a passage to elevated sensibility and irony, to the elegant charm of an ethereal elegant muse, to the breath-taking beauty of mademoiselle *Tristesse*. I too have my little semi-abandoned church in a yard where I sit to contemplate the shimmering dust: the Anglican Church in Southwark, South London, in a small street at the corner of Abbeville Road. There I sat on the cold stone just the other day, my monkish head in my hands, contemplating through warm tears a distant conversation with summer in its full idiotic swing: *I love you and love your madness... May God (who doesn't exist) help us...* Not a single voice now in the empty streets. God is dead and I miss him. I miss his terrestrial shadows – love above all, love as lightning in the counterfeit summer sky. *May God help us!* Yes, I love your folly and do not fear it. What scares me is the folly of realistic reason, the folly that changes an angel into a common-sense devil. The angel is after all only a devil who had no chance to think. The devil, supreme in the world abandoned by God, similar in his destiny to Hermes, raped by technology: our love, 80% virtual – the virtues of love killed by virtual reality. Such virtues thrived on distance, on the inalienable alterity of the other. The imaginary bridge erected by Hermes' glistening knick-knacks finally broke Aphrodite, demolished Salmacis' fountain, no longer quenching the travellers' thirst. Tourists take snapshots of the ruins and contemplate the assembling dust. The virtual dimension made us immune to the fruitful ache of distance... The cybernetic era in which we live and breathe has changed the heart of Hermes, once winged-messenger of the gods. Well-equipped with the tools of technology, indoctrinated by the new ideology (the medium is the message etc.) they foolishly convinced him that he himself is the supreme god. Co-opted by police surveillance, by plots of dystopia, by a Brave New World where everyone is linked to everyone else, available and easily reachable 24/7, a world where everyone is more and more alone. The ubiquity of a demonic Hermes in the grip of hubris and of a fantasy of omnipotence has destroyed Love. Love rests on the unknown, on the unknowability of the other. It's impossible to love one we believe we know fully. To say *I love you* means affirming at the same time *I don't know you*.

From the ruins of love we move in haste. Yet among the mutilated statues in the temple, among the weeds of sensuality which strangled the wild flowers of tenderness I tonight choose to wonder. Not in order to decode its mystery, but to honour its immaculate distance.

Eros works with Psyche, both synchronized by the system of systems, the nervous system. Their solidarity touches the chords of a secret harmony, but in most beings the allegiance is short-lived. For the tiny winged fairy it is impossible to host in her heart more than one emotion at any given time. Perhaps what truly matters is not what we seek but what we find. We have to seek only to find something unexpected. Is this the subtlety of imaginary teleology, free from the anxiety of devouring Kronos? Time is not money, but wine matured in the barrel, no frills vintage wine. A man who has lived through the seasons is a gift to his woman. And even if we uproot the vine and fly off into the wide world, roving and free, we still feel the atavistic pull. The sight of Italy provokes in me spontaneous feelings which I have no control over. I held back the tears seeing Rome's lights during take-off. Nevermore...*never more*... The raven's shadow on the floor... This endless night... No more words. Nevermore... I stutter like an idiot, and stuttering might well be the beginning of poetry. The airport at sunset. Nevermore. *Never more*...

We write for the dead. Was Genet right?

We write in order to survive, as Wordsworth did in the cruel winter of 1798 in Goslar, Low Saxony, blocked for four months by bad weather in an uncomfortable dwelling, discovering the extraordinary in the ordinary, the epic in the everyday, awakening to a non-virtual reality. The telephone itself is virtual, so goes the argument, and so is television. I remember a New Year's Eve watching supermodels and singers drinking champagne on TV on a floodlit stage of hopeless jollity and we too uncorking a bottle filling our glasses. Then my aunt looks at me lovingly and says out of the blue *How hideous death truly is...someone disappears forever and all you're left with is a handful of memories...*

Nevermore says Edgar Poe's raven, sinister shadow on a cold kitchen floor. The path of liberation is painful; we are torn from the soil, from loved ones who want to shield us from the horizon. And yet sometimes I feel I would gladly trade my freedom for the illusory warmth of ancestral ties. The bodhisattva path is hard. We grow fond of ties – of chains even – and end up loving the walls of our prison.

I dreamt of coming down stone stairs in a new morning, opening the piano and playing the notes of a song written on a distant summer. I dreamt of an abandoned piano out of tune with a red cloth covering the keys. A woman sitting on the floor like a child listens to the shaky chords.

The path of liberation is hard, and the crow perched on the fence in the cold sun repeats nevermore, *never more*. I resist the ancient call and renew my face, the face of an exile: I don't believe Italian melodies, the melodramas of clammy emotions; I don't believe the S.O.S of vain regret. I despise the small-minded Italy of Pavarottis and Jovanottis, of mascarpone and panettone; I hate the bloody sentimentality, the racism against the gypsies and the *sans papiere*, I can't stand its bigotry, the trendy drugs that keep models thin and ridiculed by Italy's sadistic designers. I don't believe your little tunes o land of my birth nor your emotional gesturing your inebriated pseudo-compassion; can't stand the sickening symbiosis of your single mothers softly strangling their male children. I hate your mamma myths, devouring, seducing, poisoning mamma, inevitable as fate according to Dr. Carl Gustav Jung. But I don't give a damn, mamma my foot, mamma dancing on my grave, bound like the deadly ballast that will pull you down and make you drown. Here, I give you a sacrificial gift, mamma whore – I'll distract from your ever-present and famished torment and I'll escape your claws. O yes I have discovered something more powerful than you, I have discovered art and poetry, here I offer it to you as a gift, mother of the gilded shiny corn fields, fertile mother dancing on the rope stretched between one season and the next. Thanks to poetry I am no longer your slave – mother lover Italian woman, green-eyed Aphrodite manufactured by technology, but surely an avatar of Aphrodite is not the goddess herself but a pathetic winged fairy unable to contain in her soul more than one feeling at a time hence a poor male child is subject to the martyrdom of her mood swings, and a lover, my God a lover is truly lost.

But it's not permitted, no sir, in the tower of song it is

simply not allowed to be ruined by a woman. I work in that tower you see, I am a jester, a troubadour, o yes I'm a singing philosopher and they simply won't allow a woman to slaughter me. And that pathetic voodoo toy you use to exercise the waning powers of your hatred, well it doesn't have the slightest resemblance to the undersigned I dare say, for *I is another* and so, my dear Italian mamma, I send you straight to hell.

The baby falcon flew away from the church desecrated by my presence. It flew away, the baby falcon, free to roam in the Presbyterian northern skies, away from Pavarottis and Jovanottis, away from a putrefying and double-breasted suit *cavaliere*. O land of my birth, laughingstock of Europe you've got the rulers you deserve but I am free from the claws of the falconer, from the motherly claws of a fatuous and vicious homeland, and this freedom is the fate of every lucky son who wriggles out of the amorous castrating clasp and stops carrying blood-dripping trophies snatched from the blue expanse to be brought to the feet of his mummy his sweet and tender little mummy, no more gifts torn from the ribs of the infant and pubescent male. The cord is busted the chain is broken the falcon is free, the male falcon is free, he is free at last.

* * *

My coarse and bitter freedom... Running, I barely dodged in the dusty wind all the pathetic statues made of salt and finally stopped at the edge of the blue planet to contemplate its sunsets.

Nevermore, never more.

Sure I wouldn't mind at times being a Casanova, a Don Juan, just for the hell of it, or out of suave aesthetic cruelty of intents. But I fall in love each time and the heart breaks in the gray autumn air, listening to the ancient refrain of abandonment and separation. Listen to me, Doc: my mother died when I was nineteen. It happened in March; the sea took her and I couldn't save her. So I went wide-eyed into the wide world in search of fortune, up and down, Doctor, through the Presbyterian North where they make love without fuss, they do it, how can I put it, efficiently; in Northern Europe where one gets drunk on Friday nights after a forty hour working week. And each time the heart crumbles, at each departure bleeding the pain of farewells. Each time a symphony in a minor key on the waves of a transit tears my rib, as with my own hand I reach the heart right into the bones of my ribcage as a pagan Calabrian Christ, Doc, a Calabrian Christ but adopted by merciful London town.

Damn it I had it here, a permit that'd ship me from life to death and back, I did have it, I am telling you, right here in my retina the blasted image that protects me on the journey to the other shore. Kanzeon, Quan-Yin or the Virgin Mary, if you must. I have no age-of-Enlightenment qualms, Doctor, oh no, not me, incense smoke does not upset my nostrils in the least. And I have travelled, I've seen a bit of the world you know, loved women who loved me back. And I do love the distant love for yes I do the distant love for whom no song or sonata was composed, the love for whom no dance was choreographed. My mother vanished in the waves and my adolescent arms could not save her and I am still not hopeless enough to renounce the very idea of salvation.

Death, anxiety and despair you say? But nowadays the real challenge is to be able to speak to a person in the flesh at the customer-service department of the local branch of your bank or pay your bills on time and resist the ever-present pull to go up and up along the staircase of private property's rosy happiness. Grand themes, great thinkers you say? But those are luxuries of a bygone era… This pair of buffoons you see, the Socrates/Plato double act, the standup comedians whose routine is devotedly recycled at the turn of every bloody century by new gray eminences – this pair of cheap clowns to whom we owe our chronic self-created disappointment, the nightmare from which no civil war will ever awake us: history. In the Italian language (the bemused English-speaking world point out) the word used to describe events – war, devastations and coronations – is the same as the one used to describe a tale, a fable and a fiction: *storia*. Could it be that the Italian language has inherited by mistake the profound frivolity of the ancient Greeks?

* * *

Cancel my subscription to the resurrection Jim Morrison sang already in 1967. I would add, forty-one years on: cancel my subscription to the idolatry of salvation. And now that you are at it, cancel my subscription to homeostasis, to the wellbeing of accountants, to therapized equilibrium, to the very idea of happiness. Cancel my subscription to Buddhist enlightenment, to so-called spiritual awakening. Cancel my subscription to philosophy, metaphysics, to the very idea that something or other is keeping the whole show going. Cancel my subscription to psychotherapy and counseling. Cancel even my subscription to such negation in which I disport myself on an autumn night, having realized with some anxiety that I have used up all my savings – spent in search of joys and vain certainties, spent between survival and the regality of a risible yet graceful existence under the cloudy sky.

On a cold autumn day I sipped red wine with an old friend – both of us straight out of a Beckett drama, coming out of two white sacs and with different illusions in our skulls. We both watch buses dashing by in the cold in a town where every road is obstinately without her. Alone later from the upper deck of the 24 bus at Camden Town I put my monkish head in my hands to hide the tears.

* * *

The daily exodus from the everyday towards the virtual world is denigration of the ordinary. Its antidote is the *magnificat* of the commonplace with Joyce as a comic celebrant and Wordsworth a meticulous one, Wordsworth who deserves among English literati the epithet of genius as Joyce wrote in a letter to his brother Stanislaus in 1905. From the splendour of the everyday (revealed to those who meditate, who are absorbed by work and love and can appreciate the uncertainty of life on the poor crust of the blue planet) flee those who manufacture a pathetic virtual avatar, bloodless and unable to sweat and build around it Hollywood and Tuscan landscapes with oriental statuettes, swimming pools and silver fountains. Wordsworth deserves the attribute of genius, Joyce said, because just like good old Giacomo Joyce adopted by Trieste he saw the extraordinary in the ordinary, the epic in the day-by-day. Joyce's letter was written in 1905. Only three years later an earthquake razed the Sicilian town of Messina to the ground. The town Nietzsche had loved was buried under the rubble. Of his *Dionysus Dithyrambs* I sense the distant hum in the radiant air, this air without you; without you and yet so merry.

Allow me to explain: your arrival was an ordinary event, but I need words and colours unknown to me to portray the visionary exhaustion that seized me when I was faced with your solitude, to paint the tenderness I felt for your little one, his tender life bound to yours, to spell out the plea you both sent out to me, the echo of you two bound to each other and turned towards me, to the life of a wanderer called to halt and worship your solitudes and become *con-sort*, sharing a fate through thick and thin. But I'm raving... The pain will surely serve *some* purpose, if it's true that Fritz wrote *Zarathustra* as an alternative to suicide, if it's true that gold materializes from raw metals, that the lotus flower comes out of the mud, I mean the flower of the Buddha who praised with Joyce and Wordsworth the extraordinary beauty of the ordinary, as testified in the erotic scriptures of Molly Bloom, worthy of the Sermon of the Mount *wild flower of the mountain mmh yes the power of a woman's' body* if memory doesn't fail me. Molly's monologue worthy of the Buddha for in its own mischievous ways it moves the Dharma wheel, which is nothing but dust and pure light, and to these dust particles swiveling in the moonlight I prostrate 108 times, and in the dust I seek refuge, in the dust and in the three Dharma jewels.

Why then rely on virtual relationships? A universe as ancient as Plato's republic, a fenced universe, divided between us and them, enemies and friends. Exiles roam outside its walls, outside the wall of an enclosed world, privileged, delusional. Beware of exiles and rebels: they dream up utopias; they'll end up choreographing new dictatorships. Utopia is by definition a place that doesn't exist. Hermes, empowered by information technology, helps us build what is not meant to come into existence, for instance the dream of love initiated in the garden of daily life. And in doing so he destroys its fundamental prerequisite: vulnerability.

The old dream of capitalism disguised as the new frontier, with the help of technology: a comfy life, armchair safaris galore. Come along, buy something, it's two for the price of one. If you resist the universal panacea, the charge against you will read: affected by mood disorder, prone to doubts engendered by low self-esteem. But to the negative faculty of doubt we owe our blossoming as a species.

We run away from love's liabilities, from sweat and tears,

we run upwards and onwards towards the toyshop, a skype camera, the image of a virtual avatar. The disappointed lover says to her man: *I thought you'd hold me if I fell, but you can't even hold yourself.* The man replies: *He saved others, he can't save himself* (Matthew, XV, 41).

Love grows after the journey through vulnerability, through the pain of a finite and imperfect being. Descending the mountain, back from the weekend's peak experiences, we renew the tenderness of the dark earth and the sweet tears of things. We are discontinuous beings, broken at the source.

The lovers' meeting place is now a pile of rubble. A fire destroyed it. How can I describe the ecstasy of love now that it feels so remote? Each pleasant sensation dissolves at the observer's touch, but here's the good news: this is also true for pain. Through observation each sensation has room to breathe. Thirty years of studying and practicing meditation did not make me happier; instead, the primary, immutable pain has found some room to breathe. I respect those who look for happiness in Buddhism and sincerely hope they'll find it. I had a formula once; I wrote it down on a piece of paper, but it got lost inside this mess. Buddhist practice is now to me a method of inquiry rather than a strategic plan for escape from *samsara*. Impermanence confirms the tragic nature of existence, roused by pathos, moistened by the tears of things. The artist has at her disposal two means: irony and pathos. Those who tend towards irony often deride pathos and keep aloof from its intensity, tiptoeing around extravagant emotions. At the genius of irony one arrives via the pain of disappointment – via an overdose of pathos, but irony is normally married to the dullest cynicism. A genius of irony – Rabelais, Joyce, Nabokov – resists the temptation of cynicism. Those inclined towards pathos and prepared to pursue its hellish path without compromise eventually come to rest within tragic joy. Our era praises objective distance and the false superiority of sarcasm. It praises irony without grasping its active pessimism, content with its passive form, typical of those who have seen their feeble dreams disintegrate with the first breeze.

Because superficial irony (nurtured by pseudo-science, inflated by cybernetics) casts a shadow on our so-called postmodern era, it colours any practice or thought that might be genuinely *other*. This is how Buddhism is apprehended: not as daring existential quest or a rigorous asking of questions to which there cannot be an answer, not as radical appreciation of impermanence, but instead as path towards happiness, catechistic absorption in exotic pseudo-answers...Buddhism as the exotic branch of the Disney store.

Impermanence reveals the tragic nature of existence. What if impermanence itself is liberation? This is the radical contribution of Zen: loss, mourning, separation felt as liberation. I am no longer the person who woke up yesterday morning. Each thing slips away and every moment I breathe a new and free existence. I do not 'truly' exist; hence I am free to create myself, provided I do not know who I might become. To this freedom and non-attachment we arrive through an excess of love. The pseudo-radicalism of those who use Zen to exhibit an iconoclastic infantilism has precious little to do with the teachings of Zen, a teaching that is radical because in love with the world, radical because it is not religion but art, a deeply *affirmative art*.

This life is a dewdrop, and yet...

We arrive at the fierce weightlessness of Zen having miraculously survived Saint Sebastian's martyrdom. Not before. Zen ordination is being ordained to a homeless existence. Sky above my head, naked earth at my feet. Only on the surface such initiation resembles being *thrown* into Heidegger's icy sidereal 'being'. Heidegger's neutral being is an abstraction, an anti-hyperbole, a professorial equation.

Grafted into the elemental kernel through hearth and dwelling: growing up in their proximity we sigh with pleasure or gloom. Before being able to dance, one learns how to walk.

* * *

By *absorbing* an event, pleasant or unpleasant, the event becomes experience. By declaring that I have desired such experience, I embrace it fully. Resentment, sorrow, pain and nostalgia become the sap that spurs me towards the future. I am grateful to the nameless melancholy that greets me unexpectedly on Monday mornings in autumn, grateful to the sense of displacement and the farewell whose trail is a faint song. I am grateful to this sadness because now I can give it a liquid face and a name: distant love, impossible love.

The dawn would kill me if it didn't live already within my heart. I am its accomplice and I invite the visible. I wait with reverence for light's nimble steps. I await the vision of an ancient song, *dawn*. Part of me rebels, vacillating in Mnemosyne's damp dark wood of reverie.

Light filters through subdued, irresistible. A hushed lament of joy.

The promise is uncertain, unreliable. Even the idea of a ray of light dissolves the shadow…

In the darkest hour the steps of dawn.

The last fragment of the mosaic is complete: I am fate's accomplice. Grateful to each lover who broke my heart, for a broken heart is an open heart, open to the fragile beauty of the world.

Thank you for disappearing over the horizon.

In the darkest hour the raven is preparing to fly away – away from my room and gone for good. Never more? *Never more*. That's good. I am fate's accomplice. I *am* fate.

The train left and the station turned black & white.
Eurydice wanders happily in the realm of the shadows.

The cage is empty and the baby falcon has become an eagle.

Morning's first light, sounds from the drowsy street.

I open the curtains to the day and I smile in the midst of
tears at the miracle: the autumn rain has turned to snow.

PERFECT
EDGE
BOOKS

"There are many who dare not kill themselves for fear of what
the neighbours will say," Cyril Connolly wrote, and we believe
he was right.
Perfect Edge seeks books that take on the crippling fear of other
people, the question of what's correct and normal, of how life
works, of what art is.
Our authors disagree with each other; their styles vary as widely as
their concerns. What matters is the will to create books that won't be
easy to assimilate. We take risks, not for the sake of risk-taking, but for
the things that might come out of it.